The New Life was published in January 1963 in the Leningrad literary monthly Neva. Russians read it, in the words of Time magazine, with "shocked incredulity." It gives to the world the first fully realistic picture, in fictional form, of the conditions on a Soviet collective farm.

Abramov takes Russia's farm problem out of the realm of statistics, and describes how it shows itself in the life of human beings. "Written with quiet humor, keen observation, and a sort of understatement," says George Reavey in his introduction, "Abramov's The New Life is an unexpectedly sensational account of both rural Russia and the Soviet collective system superimposed upon it."

The author, Fyodor Abramov, is unknown in the West. He is an editor of Neva, and has previously written another book about life in northern Russia.

The New Life

A Day
on a Collective Farm

Fyodor Abramov

*Translated and with
an Introduction by*

George Reavey

A Black Cat 🐱 *Book*

GROVE PRESS, INC.   NEW YORK

CONTENTS

INTRODUCTION

by

George Reavey

The Individual and the Collective

A note of mingled anguish, restlessness, and affirmation pervades most of the best Russian poetry since 1955. This post-Stalinist mood is well expressed by Evgeny Evtushenko in his lines, "Let us be extremely outspoken, and tell the truth concerning ourselves." The same is also true of certain Soviet writers of fiction, memoirs, and reportage. These prose writers, older men like Ehrenburg and Paustovsky, or younger men like Nekrasov, Aksionov and Solzhenitzyn, are now attempting to enlarge the frontiers of Soviet reality, which had become frozen by the too rigid application of doctrinal "socialist realism." These writers, though perhaps less anguished than the poets, are striving with greater irony and command of bare fact to fill in the gaps with suppressed detail. They are, in fact, trying to restore to Russian realism some of the vigor and reputation it had once enjoyed. But their task is not merely an aesthetic one; it has also a significant ethical bearing. They are rediscovering the concept of "truth," which had for decades been sacrificed to political expediency and party control. That some very real divergence of opinion has indeed occurred is, perhaps, best exemplified by the very recent measures (December 1962-May 1963) instigated by Mr. Khrushchev and his idealogical henchman, Mr. Ilyichev, to reassert party control over writers and artists of all sorts.

Fyodor Abramov's *The New Life: A Day On A Collective Farm,* first published in the January issue of the Leningrad magazine, *Neva,* is a work in the new revelatory mood. It is a work of refreshing, almost naive but effective realism directed toward the hitherto elusive facts of Soviet life—in this case, the Russian countryside of the collective farm. Abramov touches upon that very sensitive area of Soviet agriculture with which Mr. Khrushchev is so vitally concerned and of which he usually speaks in terms of statistics, as he has recently done to an Italian journalist: "It is not clear to what agricultural crisis you refer." (See the *New York Times*, April 22, 1963.)

Abramov, on the contrary, deals with human beings, with the peasants, kolhoz workers, and the party "managers" responsible for implementing the collective policy. Abramov has selected the simplest of themes: a kolhoz chairman, Anany Yegorovich—the hero with an almost innocent eye—who is faced with both the ruin of his crops and the uncooperative attitude of the kolhoz workers who, lacking sufficient collective incentive or gain and no longer moved by propaganda, are more concerned with the possibilities of private endeavor. This simple but fundamental issue reveals all the complexities of a system which appears inhuman and wasteful in practice.

Written with quiet humor, keen observation, and a sort of understatement, Abramov's *The New Life* is an unexpectedly sensational account of both rural Russia and the Soviet collective system superimposed upon it. The facts as presented by Abramov show not only a strong upsurge of individualism among the rural population, but also some uncertainty on the part of "the authorities." The realities of Russian life as depicted in *The New Life* are startling and give food for thought. In this sense, Abramov's work is one of the most vivid and telling accounts of "ordinary" Soviet life I have come across. In addition to the wealth of information it provides about the Russian countryside, *The New Life* also offers us an extraordinary gallery of Russian country characters, who are all determined to survive through thick and thin. The chairman Anany Yegorovich, though imbued with a sort of post-Stalin humanism, which makes him reflect on the "crimes" of the past, has moments of almost regretting the 1930's when harsher measures could be applied to a recalcitrant population.

Thus: "Anany Yegorovich bit his lower lip in indecision. Should he try and catch up with them, knock over those damn baskets, seize the women by the scruff of their necks and push them straight into the fields? Yes, some eight years ago he would certainly have done so. There were models to imitate in both life and literature. One of the books, for example, related how one kolhoz chairman used to catch uncooperative kolhoz workers outside the village, while another chairman had acted even more drastically: he'd break into a cottage in the morning and douse the stove with water. In the region these books were used for moral rearmament. 'That's how you should work,' the district committee secretary would lecture the kolhoz chairmen, quoting literary examples to illustrate every case. 'You clumsy louts, you can't even manage women.'

"Yes, some eight years ago Anany Yegorovich would have put fear into these mushroom-pickers. But now. . . ."

THE NEW LIFE

*In memory of my brother
Michael, a regular kolhoz
worker*

First Telephone Call:

"*Anany Yegorovich? Greetings, greetings. Well, and what's the good news? Very active, you say? Everyone out reaping? Very good, very good. And how is it with the silage? Getting on with it? Well, get on with it, get a move on.*"

Second Telephone Call:

"*I see no silage in the report. Your kolhoz is pulling the whole region back. What? Weather's dry, you say, and you're getting on with the hay? Get on with it, then, get on.*

19

But remember, the district committee isn't going to pat you on the head for holding off on the green feeds. Maybe they'll make an exception, but you really ought to know the political line about this."

Yes, he did know the political facts of the region well enough (thank God, he'd been an active drudge in the region for the past thirty years now): according to the report, the storage of fodder must not lag behind the hay harvest. But, the devil take it, didn't the kolhoz workers have to use their brains, too, even once in a while? At their general meeting, the kolhoz workers had decided to hold off with the fodder. They could store the fodder even in wet weather when it was impossible to harvest the hay.

Third Telephone Call:

"Comrade Mysovsky? [A form of address boding no good.] How do you want me to interpret your stubbornness? As sabotage? Or as pig-headed lack of understanding of the basic economic problem?"

"And anyway," Anany Yegorovich could not restrain himself from saying, *"who's boss in the kolhoz? The Party has now given the kolhozes their freedom, but you're again putting spokes in the wheels . . ."*

And Here's The Resolution:

1. For having politically underrated fodder as the foundation of kolhoz cattle breeding, it has been resolved to administer a severe reprimand to A. Y. Mysovsky, the chairman of the kolhoz "New Life."

2. To oblige Comrade Mysovsky to liquidate within five days the intolerable lag on the part of kolhoz "New Life" in the storage of green fodder.

I.

"Splosh-sh, splosh-sh, splosh-sh . . ."

That was underfoot, and buckets of rain kept pouring from above. And that had gone on for two weeks solid.

Anany Yegorovich had a toothache, and he walked along with the collar of his overcoat raised and his hand supporting his right cheek. Klavdia Nekhoroshkova, the brigadier of the Zarechic brigade, strode ahead of him. Her long mud-spattered raincoat stood about her as stiffly as a stake.

They both stopped near the lake.

"This is how we'll do it," said Anany Yegorovich, repeating what he'd already told her a half hour before in the office. "You'll send the tractor across the river, and then transport the silage by tractor."

"I get it," Klavdia said in a husky voice heavy with a cold.

With the palm of her hand she wiped her red, fair-browed face, and shaking herself as noisily as a horse, set off to the right, round the lake, toward the spot where the road turned in the direction of the ferry.

Anany Yegorovich began to look for the ford.

And there he was standing in the meadow. Standing as if it was torture. The rain made a dull rustling sound as it dripped down from his raincoat; the numbed hand he pressed to his cheek was getting wet; and all around him, wherever you looked, spread the *ruin of the hay harvest*. Over a hundred acres of hay were rotting outside the village and a hundred and seventy more along more distant streams.

With his boot he turned over a layer of hay —the heavy, heady scent of rotting manure struck his nostrils—and glanced up at the sky. There was not one break in those lowering, water-logged clouds. Yes, another couple of days and you might as well write off the hay. It would mean the complete ruin of the kolhoz . . .

No, he made no attempt to justify himself. It was he, Anany, who had given orders to switch the men from the hay gathering while

the weather was still dry. And he had to
press his point. He'd driven into town to inter-
district headquarters and fought for the truth
—the district committee was not the only body
over him! But, on the other hand, the kolhoz
women were a fine lot too! What were they
thinking about? Once there had been a holdup
with the hay, it would seem obvious to get a
move on with the fodder—the weather had
nothing to do with that. But they had balked
like a lot of stupid sheep—till you had to drag
them at the end of a rope. And this day, too,
the milkmaids were the only women out in the
rain in the field, where they had been getting
in the pea harvest (he'd already seen the field
from the slope a long while ago).

"Anany Yegorovich!" the milkmaids called
out in variously pitched voices when they
caught sight of him.

He waved his hand and quickened his pace.
But his heart warmed a little. It was with the
milkmaids that he had a language in common.
Seven young girls, fresh from the school bench,
and it was really on them that the whole
kolhoz depended. Every kopeck in the kolhoz
was milked by their hands.

The milkmaids!—that was perhaps the great-
est obstacle he had encountered since be-
coming chairman. The elderly kolhoz women
on whose shoulders had rested all the hard-

ships of the postwar confusion had now faded
away: the hands of one were deformed by
rheumatism; another had developed a hernia;
a third—some other ailment. Yes, and how
could you get a sharp increase in farm output
with these half-literate women; all they knew
was how to pitch hay, in the ancient way, for
the cattle. So you had to round up the senior
schoolgirls and keep them at it for weeks and
months on end. If a girl herself was willing,
her mother would be up in arms. What?
Have my daughter raking manure? Was it for
this that the old man and me broke our backs
so she could get an education?

But even after the girls had started working,
the grief they'd made him swallow! To milk
the cows, clear the manure, drive to the
meadow for fodder—these things they'd all do
willingly. But to mate a bull and a cow, let's
say. . . . Valya Postnikova, a white-skinned,
blue-eyed girl, was now working for her second year in the barnyard, but just try and tell
or show her that a sterile cow was a plague on
the kolhoz—it was all no use. Anany Yegorovich waxed indignant. What were they teach-
ing in the schools? For whom were they
turning out these young muslin ladies. All the
same, somewhere in his soul he understood
and sympathized with their shyness and
timidity.

26

The girls gathered round him on every side as soon as he set foot in the field—drenched, smiling, unusually brightly clad: one in a bright-colored raincape, another in a quilted coat, a third in colored ski pants, while Nyura Yakovleva wore just a knitted blouse. Nyura had high, shapely breasts and, one must suppose, this circumstance had a bearing of no small importance on her choice of costume.

The girls greeted him with smiles, but their talk soon turned to grumbling:

"Where are the rest of the people?"

"Is this just for the benefit of us milkmaids?"

"Why do we get all the heavy work? Are we made of steel?"

Anany Yegorovich joked back—the filthiest job of all was to play the confident man when you should be raising the roof! Then, hearing a sputtering sound in the meadow, he deflected the girls' attention to the machine.

Vasska Ouledev, thrusting his hook-nosed, bandit's mug out the driver's cab, was backing his truck down the field.

"Everything O.K.," he reported, jumping out. "Chugayev's at the ditch with three women."

"And why isn't Yakov here?"

"Yashka's got stuck in the stream. His brakes failed."

Ouledev spoke sideways. His wild, tar-black, protruding eyes had a suspicious gleam.

27

"Have you been hitting the bottle this morning?"

Vasska frowned, pushed back his red beret stained with oil, but he could not lie:

"Only the weak stuff. I'm still off the hundred proof vodka!"

"Look here, Ouledev. If I catch you again, it will mean your discharge. It's the last time I'm warning you."

"Well, Anany Yegorovich, they used to allow us a good regular portion during the war, but here. . . . And think of the weather. If I drop out . . ."

Anany Yegorovich stopped listening. The girls were already loading the truck. He picked up a spare pitchfork—a three-pronged one— and buckled down to helping them. The pea pods were large and fuzzy. Whenever he raised a heap of them, torrents of water gushed down, and some of it found its way under his collar. From time to time he encouraged the girls:

"That's the way, girls! Very good!"

"Come on, come on, girls! Put more joy into it!" Vasska urged them, following Anany's example. "Your bridegrooms are watching you from the village."

Someone crowned him with a heap of pea pods from behind. Vasska yelled and swore and began running around the field. But it was a joke, and it all ended in laughter.

The truck was rapidly loaded, and then they had to push against the body to get it out into the meadow, for the wheels slithered, spun, and mired up to their axles.

There was still no sign of Yakov, the second truck driver. He must have got stuck for good. Nor were the kolhoz workers in any hurry to get to the field. Whitish smoke curled here and there above the high, bush-covered slope, on which the village stood out like a hump. Let the hay go to ruin, let the peas rot—we're heating our bathhouse. In the middle of the day too.

While waiting for the second truck, the girls bunched together on firmer ground at the edge of the field. Nyura Yakovleva, twitching her chilled little shoulders, began to shake off sticky bits of green from her beautiful knitted blouse.

"Come here, under my raincape, Nyura, or you'll freeze," offered Elsa, the milkmaids' brigadier.

"I wouldn't do that! You're frozen yourself," Nyura replied.

Brave girl! There was no point whining. Yes, it was wonderful to see the young ones. Not so long ago the mother of this very same Nyura had lamented to him: "What sort of a cow girl would she make? Do you think she could even carry a bucket of water? Just look at her breasts, they haven't developed yet." But she was a fine girl now. Strong, with white teeth, and dimples in her firm, tanned cheeks. But how long would she stay on in the kolhoz? Girls like her are picked up very quickly. All right if she married one of her own folk, a villager. But what if she got carried off elsewhere? Then they'd have to try and find another milkmaid.

The girls began singing some new song unfamiliar to Anany Yegorovich. A song about Vanya-the-pilot and Marussia-the-betrayer. But the song did not warm up. The rain squelched it.

They loaded two more trucks.

Anany Yegorovich, deep in thought, stared at the village. Now smoke was rising all over the slope. What a lot these peasants were! Just try and raise the standard of the kolhoz with the likes of them. And the brigadiers too. Where the devil had the brigadiers got lost?

Gusts of wind reached them from over the river. The wet cape of a poisonous blue color, which the milkmaids held over their heads, flapped noisily above them.

"How goes it, girls? Aren't you frozen?"

A stupid question! Why ask it, if he himself was chilled to the bone.

In the end he signaled with his hand. Time to go home. They might, of course, load another couple of trucks before mealtime, but two more truckfuls would not solve anything, and the milkmaids might catch cold.

And there he was again, all alone with his grief. The peas were being drowned in the dumps on the field; the hay was rotting in the meadows. . . .

After thinking for a while he walked toward the river. Ten days had passed since he had last been to see the Zarechie brigade working on the other bank under the direction of Klavdia Nekhoroshkova and, if he found the boat, now would be the best time for him to go over there.

But the boat was on the other bank.

A path had been beaten from the boat landing to the house on the edge of the embankment. It was Klavdia's path, or Klavdia's "little trail," as it was called in the kolhoz. A beaten track, it had been hacked out, as straight as Klavdia herself, from the yellow sandy earth.

For nineteen years Klavdia had trampled out her path. You'd gaze in the early morning in the direction of Zarechie—the sun would just be blinking its eyes and Klavdia would already be on the move. Tall and majestic she was, like that female giant of the folk tales,

31

and she wore her white kerchief like a sail. But in foul weather, when the savage wind pressed all living creatures down to the earth, Klavdia resembled a she-bear just roused from her lair.

Even in wintertime she kept no one waiting. Whatever might be going on outside—crackling frost, blinding blizzard such as prevented the Zarechie folk, who had been huddling for weeks in their homes, from crossing over to the village—Klavdia would get on her skis and start treading her path again. Another time she would burst into the manager's office—through the drifts of snow with no trace of life anywhere around—and then her chilled voice could be heard asking as from the bottom of a well: "What are your orders, chairman?"

Nevertheless, Klavdia had been demoted from brigadier at least ten times, and even now she was officially listed as a mere "temporary deputy." For bad work? For lack of organization? On the contrary: the Zarechie brigade was always first on the list, and there was no point in discussing Klavdia as a worker —she got on with people and did a man's work no worse than any man, and, in a case of extreme necessity, she could be relied upon to get behind the wheel of a tractor. No, it was not for inefficient work that Klavdia got demoted, but for that very same beaten path of

hers along which she strode not only to the
kolhoz office, but also in some other directions.
An outstanding worker in the kolhoz, she was
also its outstandingly free and easy woman. . . .
You might, indeed, scratch your head when
the time came to draw up the balance sheet
for the year.

When it was time to award the red banner,
who'd you give it to? To a woman against
whom up to a dozen complaints had been
filed in the chairman's office? They had tried
everything: to shame her, to persuade her;
they had even appointed a man to replace her
as brigadier. But what man could stand being
in her shoes for long? And so once again,
against their will, they had called in Klavdia.
"Take on the brigade, Nekhoroshkova just for
a while, of course."

Anany Yegorovich stood for a long minute or
two on the steep river bank. Waves were rolling over the river, and the slanting rain
thrashed him—but not a person was to be seen
on the other bank. Where were all the people?
In the fields beyond the houses? But why was
there no sound of a tractor? It was Saturday,
an ordinary weekday—God Himself com-
manded them to work. And what would happen tomorrow, a Sunday?

No, he must do something. Do something
decisive, now. It was the middle of August—

what were they all waiting for? This is what he would do in the first place. He'd mount the hill and began sifting through the upper end of the village. He'd enter each house, get at every kolhoz worker individually. Why aren't you at the forage? How long, devil take you, are you going to play the bagpipes and do nothing else?

II. One Should Help,
But How?

The first building—a small cottage with a steep, single-sided roof (you can't miss it as you climb the slope to the village)—belonged to Avdotya Moiseyevna. It was a ramshackle little cottage. The approach to it was rather wretched and untidy; near the cottage there was a strip of white barley with a scarecrow —say what you will, it looked like a picture come alive from a pre-revolutionary magazine.

Anany Yegorovich had first run into Avdotya Moiseyevna in the street. As he was walking one morning through the village, he suddenly caught sight of an old woman standing under a window—a small, almost blind old crone, with a cane and a birch basket in her hands.

The window opened and a hand was thrust out with a morsel of bread. The old woman crossed herself, put the gifts in her basket, and hobbled off.

Anany Yegorovich was surprised. How was this? A beggar, in this day and age? Who could she be?

It turned out she had once been a kolhoz worker. Now she lived all alone. Without relatives. She did, indeed, have a son, but he had disappeared—"for talking."

On Anany Yegorovich's insistence, the kolhoz management had allocated a small pension to Moiseyevna: twenty-two pounds of grain per month, and four cartloads of logs for the winter. It was the first pension that had ever been granted in the whole existence of the kolhoz.

Moiseyevna was, of course, at home in such foul weather. She was sitting on the low threshold of a woodshed; there was a dull sound of hammering within as the rainwater spurted freely from the roof. Hearing the steps of a passerby (the path ran along the side of a fence enclosing her grounds), she raised her yellow-white eyes. A shy smile of expectation and hope froze on her slightly open, toothless mouth.

Anany Yegorovich lowered his eyes and walked past.

"Knock, knock," the small hammer sounded again. The moist air smelled of grain that had been recently dried on the top of a stove. On a wooden block Moiseyevna was threshing her first sheaf of freshly garnered barley.

Anany Yegorovich bypassed the second household in the neighborhood. A striped, rain-logged mattress was hung over the fence, and some prickly branches of juniper were stuck to the wall by the cottage steps, but the master of the house himself had been gone to the cemetery these three days. He had died of tuberculosis, choked by the August dampness.

He had been sick a long while, this Nikanor Tikhonovich. But when you still saw him among the living, he was always very busy just outside the house. He'd be doing something in the woodshed—he had helped the kolhoz now and then by providing a sledge— or he'd be mending a horse collar. For the last few weeks he hadn't been able to walk at all. But he seemed to have found it tiresome to be cooped up in the stuffy atmosphere of his cottage. So out he'd come crawling to the fence, spread a homemade mattress there, and stretch out in the sun with his eye fixed on the village road.

"How's the health, Nikanor Tikhonovich?" you'd ask him.

"Not too bad this day. I ate a little. But it's my legs I need most."

"Don't worry. It's too early for you to be thinking of the grave."

"I'm all right! Don't you worry."

He was a great optimist, he was.

Nikanor Tikhonovich left four children. His widow couldn't raise them all, not by herself. And didn't his work for the kolhoz these many years entitle him to some care for his family? A pension for them was essential. A few other people were also in need of pensions. Very soon now Anany would be passing by the house of Mikhey Lukich. Oh how his teeth were aching! Old man Lukich had passed four score and ten. He was the oldest man in the village. And now he lived like a wild beast. In the winter he slept on the stove, and never even crawled out of the house.

But, on the other hand, what was there left to spare from a kolhoz budget? In the past year they had paid out only thirty kopecks per working day and this year, for the fifth month in succession, the kolhoz workers had received no advance cash at all. There just wasn't any money! Maybe in a month's time they might get some money when their livestock had been turned over to the State Purchasing Agency. But for the present, they'd tighten the belt to the last inch.

Every ruble went into the construction of two cattle barns. They must be completed, regardless of cost, before the first snow—or the livestock would be stranded without winter quarters.

When a small neat house with white casings, inhabited by the construction brigadier, loomed in front of him, Anany Yegorovich decided to call on him too. If Voronitzin was at home—it was the midday meal time—he must have a serious chat with him. What was the matter? Construction workers were well paid—one ruble in cash plus their daily norm[1]—and still, the barn had not yet been finished. As for Voronitzin himself, lately he'd gone on the booze quite often.

[1] Percentage of produce according to the number of hours worked, stipulated in advance.

III. The Chief Support

Following the war Anany Yegorovich had become the thirteenth chairman in Bogatka. Thirteen was considered an ill-omened number among the people.

And true enough, his chairmanship had started with a conflict—not with just one or even two kolhoz workers, but with the whole of the kolhoz in one fell swoop.

It was wintertime, and the frost was savage. Assuming his kolhoz duties, he had in a single day made the round of the cattle sheds, the stables, the storage barns—a difficult inheritance all this, left him by the outgoing chairman—and that same evening he had raced to the office for his first management talk. But instead he found himself involved in a general meeting. The office was so packed with people you couldn't even squeeze your way through to the table. What was it all about? Hadn't they had enough at yesterday's general assembly?

"It's the elections for the local Soviet tomorrow," the bookkeeper informed him.

"So what?"

"So we've come for the money."

"What money?"

It turned out it was a custom of long standing to distribute an advance of ten to fifteen rubles per voter on the eve of the elections. The custom was not a bad one in itself. What sort of a holiday could you have without money? There'd be an open buffet at the club, the district center might possibly contribute some sausage, cans of meat, hard rolls, and other delicacies, in which the village was never too rich—and there you'd stand and stare with bulging eyes.

But custom is one thing; kolhoz accounts another. And Anany Yegorovich replied:

"You needn't count on it. There'll be no money."

"You won't fork over then, you mean?" This was said by a red-faced, muscular man who was sitting by the stove.

"No, I won't," Anany Yegorovich cut him short.

42

"Well, if you won't fork over, we won't vote."

"What's this—do you vote for money or for the Soviet power?"

All of a sudden, the red-faced man smiled disarmingly:

"An odd fellow you are. It's *you* we won't vote for." (Anany Yegorovich had just been nominated for the local Soviet.)

There was much sniggering and smiling.

"Whose speeches are you quoting, Voronitzin?" curtly asked Isakov, the secretary of the party organization.

Voronitzin—that was the name of the red-faced man—waved his hand lazily:

"Don't frighten me. I've been frightened before."

"He's faced a German firing squad. Have you forgotten?" someone shouted from the doorway.

After they had finally managed to get the people out of the office, Isakov clutched his head between his hands:

"Do you realize what you've done, comrade Mysovsky? You've undermined the elections. Yes, yes! Formerly we always used to report before eight o'clock, but what if no one turns up tomorrow?"

The elections went off as usual. But what an

experience it had been for Anany Yegorovich on the eve. He had even scraped the money together—he'd taken it on account from the director of the local farm co-operative. The devil take it, now that he had hustled, paid up, and run around the whole village.

And next day, a Monday it was, Voronitzin presented himself at the office early in the morning and stared at Anany a long time with laughing eyes.

"It looks as if we'll get on together, chairman," he declared as if drawing up the balance sheet of their quarrel.

Voronitzin's word turned out to be as reliable as his heavy stub-fingered hand, which wielded an ax and a smith's hammer with equal skill. In the first year he, with his brigade of carpenters, had roofed one of the cattle barns and, in the second year, he covered yet another one.

And then this same reliable man, so very essential to the kolhoz, and, it may be said, the chairman's chief support, took to drink. Anany Yegorovich tried to approach him this way and that. "Tell me, what's eating you?" he would ask. But Voronitzin just kept silent; you couldn't get a word out of him; and the completion of the barn was now in danger. Since their construction brigadier had stuck his nose in a bottle, what demands could you possibly make on the others?

The small kitchen was clouded with tobacco smoke. The white smoke hung in a thick layer beneath the low ceiling. On the table stood a samovar, a plate of rye bread and barley rusks, and an earthen pot full of curdled milk. Some five children—each smaller than the other—sat primly on the right-hand side in the space between the door opening onto the front room and the window with a white curtain through which the village street could be seen. They sat there dipping their bread into small mounds of granulated sugar heaped directly on the table in front of each of them.

The place where the master of the house usually sat—a stool by the window on the left —was empty. A tall glass of tea had not been finished. A pile of cigarette butts lay on a tray all around the legs of the samovar.

"The master not in?" asked Anany Yegorovich.

From behind a pink curtain by the stove peeped out Polina—Voronitzin's wife, a tall lean woman in a homely, quilted, sleeveless jacket and with a face flushed from the heat of the stove and ill-humored glittering eyes.

"He was here. A whole hour he sat about grunting."

"Is he sick?"

"The devil's got into him! For a whole week he's done nothing but guzzle and drink."

Anany Yegorovich, as if justifying himself, asked:

"And where does he get the money? I didn't give him any recently."

Polina snorted:

"Where does he get the money! Those damned drunkards have been living for a long time on the communist plan. It's God's truth, I tell you! They'll go into a store: 'Manka,' they'll say, 'give me half a bottle of vodka, and I'll sign for it.' And Manka—at the end of the month—tramps around the whole village, from house to house, collecting. 'From you, Polina, ten rubles and fifty kopecks!' "—Hereupon Polina, stretching out her long thin neck, demonstrated how she and Manka talked.—" 'What for? When did I spend that?' 'Your man's been taking vodka and signing for it.' 'Well, if he took it, collect from him then. You shouldn't trade on the communist plan.' "—Polina's glance darted toward the table. "See how many bread carpenters I've got?"

The children, who had been closely watching their mother who always addressed people very theatrically and bluntly, resumed their activity of dipping bread in sugar.

"Get out!" Polina shouted, suddenly descending upon them. "How much longer are you going to sit here? These brats stick to the house all day. They're getting on my nerves, the little devils."

Reluctantly the children crawled away from the table and, glaring at Anany Yegorovich, moved into the entrance hall.

"Polina Arkhipovna," said Anany Yegorovich, closing the door after them, "do you think you know what's got into him? What's driving him to drink?"

Polina sighed.

"Only the evil spirits can tell. It's since he's come back from town that all this has happened. He used to drink before—couldn't do without it, but he still knew his business. And then he came here from town—you'd say they had put another man in his place. Are you keeping your eye on things properly, you bosses?"

"All right," said Anany Yegorovich. "I'll go back now. I'll put the squeeze on him. Tell him not to go off anywhere."

IV. Times Have Changed

Outside it was exactly the same—raining; the wind tossed about the soaking wash slung over a rope. . . .

Anany Yegorovich turned with his back to the wind to light a match, and then suddenly straightened up. Along a back path, past the Voronitzins' grounds, three women came tramping. With baskets. Bent double.

"Halt there!" shouted Anany Yegorovich and immediately clapped his hand to his cheek: the cold air had blown into his mouth.

The women darted around the corner of a bathhouse.

Without picking his way, he ran through a

damp potato patch to cut them off and jumped over a fence.

"Working hard?" he asked them, choking with exertion and rage.

The women said not a word. Drenched, blue, looking crucified, they stood there with their backs propped against the bathhouse and stared dully at him. Their large wicker baskets, filled to the top with red-and-yellow mushrooms, bulked at their feet.

"Working hard, what?" Anany Yegorovich insisted.

"Well, we're not the only ones."

"If we were a kopeck the richer in the kolhoz," Argafena began in a whimpering voice, "who'd go into the forest, Anany Yegorovich?"

"And where's the kopeck to come from? Fall out of the sky?" he demanded.

The women grew bolder:

"It's the fifteenth year we're hearing that," said one. "I spent the whole of this little summer reaping—but how much did I earn?"

"And my kids will have to go to school very soon—there's nothing for shoes or clothes," said the second. "Do you think we like to wander about in the forest? The teeth just go on chattering, and there's not a dry thread left on you. And you go on wandering. Then you hand in your basket of mushrooms to the Co-op, and you have a kopeck of sorts in the house."

"And don't we ourselves have to eat?" Olena Rogaleva asked in a rough, hoarse voice, suddenly breaking into the conversation. "This is the second year I've been suffering without a cow. Now that we have a lot of hay, I thought I'd get a cow. But the devil take it, you think I'll ever get it?"

And evidently regarding any further talk superfluous, Olena picked up her baskets, the handles of which creaked, and walked off bending under the load.

Her companions followed her, one after another, their legs a little shaky.

Anany Yegorovich bit his lower lip in indecision. Should he try and catch up with them, knock over those damn baskets, seize the women by the scruff of their necks and push them straight into the fields? Yes, some eight years ago he would certainly have done so. There were models to imitate in both life and literature. One of the books, for example, told how one kolhoz chairman used to catch uncooperative kolhoz workers outside the village, while another chairman had acted even more drastically: he'd break into a cottage in the morning and douse the stove with water. At party headquarters these books were used for

51

moral rearmament. "That's how you should work," the district secretary would lecture the kolhoz chairmen, quoting literary examples to illustrate every case. "You clumsy louts, you can't even manage women."

Yes, some eight years ago Anany Yegorovich would have put fear into these mushroom-pickers. But now . . .

He raised his hand to the wet peak of his cap, pulled it sharply over his eyes, and set off, walking around the Voronitzin farmstead, toward the main street.

V. The Virus Grippe

To the left, on the other side of the road leading from the Voronitzins, on the mounds—as
they called the wasteland or vacant ground
stretching under the hillside—lived Pyotr Gavrilovich Khudyakov,

This wasteland was not even known to exist
some thirty years ago. Here, on what had been
the village outskirts, some dozen houses had
huddled very close together, almost leaning on
each other. Now only two houses had survived:
Pyotr Gavrilovich's cottage and, some two hundred yards to the left of it, a high five-walled
house without roof or windows, its black rafters
raised like an old man's arms to the sky.

Anany Yegorovich had often pondered over

the fate of this abandoned house as he walked across the wasteland. He remembered this house in its youth. Its walls of selected "ringing" pine, as they say, the corners, tarred (for Eternity)—all ready for the housewarming as soon as the window frames were fitted. But the house had aged without any housewarming. Who were its owners? Where were they now? Were they still among the living? And what had made them abandon their newly built house and not even come once to see it?

There it was, perched on a hillock, this old house, waiting day and night for its proprietors. And still the proprietors never came. . . .

Anany Yegorovich did not find it necessary to enter the farmstead. Pyotr Gavrilovich, who had just turned seventy, was sitting inside a covered woodshed, plying his ax. When he saw the chairman he stood up and walked to the gate. Pyotr Gavrilovich wore a pair of felt boots and red galoshes, quilted trousers, a jersey, and an old sweaty winter cap with ear flaps but without ties—he was dressed warmly to suit the weather. And in his mouth, ringed with thin yellow stubble, he held an immutable cigarette butt.

"Going far?" he inquired, holding out his hand. Pyotr Gavrilovich always addressed the authorities very freely, but without any insulting familiarity.

"I'm worrying about the silage. Do you realize what's happening?"

"You've got to worry," Pyotr Gavrilovich said encouragingly. "We've got stuck with this silage, comrade Myosovsky." He raised his head. "The Old Man above has let us down."

"You needn't rub it in."

"Never mind, lad. The weather looks like clearing. This wind will blow away the damp."

Anany Yegorovich followed Pyotr Gavrilovich's example and gazed up at the sky. The gray blanket there had indeed been torn in places. And the rain seemed to be slowing down.

"The wind will blow it away, it will," Pyotr Gavrilovich confirmed his prognosis with even greater certainty.

"How's the health?"

"The health, you say?" Pyotr Gavrilovich sighed and chewed his lips. His face suddenly looked martyred. "Very bad, my lad. What with the weather almost doing me in, and now with the grippe devouring me."

"Got a temperature?"

"It would be easier with one. But there's a new sort of grippe now going around. With virus. It sits inside you and doesn't show."

"All right," Anany Yegorovich said after a while. "Get better."

It would, of course, have been possible to

demonstrate to this Khudyakov just where his virus grippe had manifested itself. He, Anany Yegorovich, had noticed from the street all the improvements that had been made in the fences and the new garland carved above the cottage steps—nothing of this had been there a week ago, and, besides, to sit in a shed in such weather was not the best method of curing the grippe. But Khudyakov was an old man. And had he lived in town, what could you hold against him? But the fact that healthy peasants also worked for themselves when excused from their duties on grounds of a virus grippe was a more serious matter. Here something had to be done.

"But what?" thought Anany Yegorovich, striding along the curb of a soggy street. "What's clear is that Faina, our woman medical assistant, can't bring order into all this by herself. As it is, she examines a 'sick' man from every angle, and he seems all right judging by his symptoms. But the patient insists: 'Well, it must be the virus grippe then. Give me a certificate!' And just you try and prove that he is putting it on.

"Yes," sighed Anany Yegorovich. "Ah, this virus grippe! It's queer how often it breaks up our peasant of today. . . ."

56

VI. Pensioners' Day

"Good health to you, Anany Yegorovich."

"What's upsetting you so? Don't you look at people any more?"

Mysovsky turned his head toward the speakers.

On the other side of the street a whole company of old women was marching along in single file. They were all smartly and festively dressed—the way people used to dress when going to church.

Anany Yegorovich crossed the street.

"Where are you off to in formation?"

"What's the matter with you? This is our day," smiled a tall old woman with smooth pink cheeks, who was still strong and straight. "You should remember the date."

"Pension Day. Is that where you're going?"

"For the pension, for the pension," a little old woman in brightly colored rubber boots exclaimed, nodding her head.

"Thanks to the present authorities," said a short, stout old woman, who suddenly made a low, formal bow. "If I were literate, I'd write straight to Moscow myself. They haven't forgotten our old age."

Anany Yegorovich, as his eyes followed these briskly striding pensioners, mulled over thoughts that were far from joyful: "Ah, these old women, these old women! If only you added a little awareness to those pensions of yours. Not all of you, of course, but a few of you could still hold a rake in your hands. Then we'd see things brighten up in the kolhoz."

VII. "And Does The Earth Grow?"

The Pozdeyevs—father and son—were laboring on their new house. Old man Ignat, in an old leather coat and with a warm, faded kerchief knotted in female fashion under his bearded chin—he had long been suffering from an earache—was fixing something under the shed, while Kirka, a young man with very broad shoulders, was hewing a log with his ax. He hewed with canny dexterity. Cut one, cut two, then a wedge and a twist, and a large sliver of white-faced wood fell away cleanly from the log.

Anany Yegorovich decided not to turn and call on the Pozdeyevs. What could he get from them? Kirka, a cripple with a game leg, had

had tuberculosis of the bone since childhood. Ignat himself was well advanced in years; and, besides, to give them their due, they had done their bit of toiling at hay harvest in some of the more distant fields.

But he did not succeed in avoiding the Pozdeyevs. As if to spite him, the old man raised his head and shouted in a high-pitched, crowing voice:

"What are you poking your nose about here for? We aren't thieves."

Kirka straightened his back and, baring his strong white teeth in a smile, said:

"Humor the old man, comrade chairman."

There was nothing to be done—he had to "humor" him. It wasn't safe to joke with these Pozdeyevs: father and son shared an unusual temperament—they were both expert at starting up a public circus. Say there is a lecture on the international situation at the club. One man listens, another dozes, a third near the door chatters his head off. And then, suddenly, an old man in a woman's kerchief jumps up in the front row and asks: "Hey, tell me, does the earth grow?"

The district lecturer doesn't know what to answer. What does this question have to do with the current imperialist exploitations! But unwilling to offend the inquisitive old man, he begins to explain in popular fashion all about the law of the conservation of matter.

"It doesn't grow, you say?" Ignat demands, jumping to his feet again. "And have you been to our cleared lands?[1] You never used to see a single stone in the field, and now the plow bounces off them. Where did the stones come from then, if the earth doesn't grow?"

There is noise, laughter, and a lot of squealing in the hall.

Then people quiet down and the lecture continues. In a little while Ignat's voice is heard again:

"Don't get it! What's he muttering like a deacon!"

This time, freeing his ear from the kerchief, he turns to his son who always sits beside him.

Kirka, pleased to carry out the duties of an interpreter, announces:

"He's talking about the harvest."

"About the harvest? Ah, about the harvest!" says Ignat, getting heated. "Then answer," he shouts again at the lecturer, "what's more profitable to plant—a birch tree or grain?"

The interpreter, wishing to help out the lecturer, bawls in the old man's ear:

"The question is not clear!"

"Not clear?" Now Ignat completely loses control of himself. "What the fucking hell . . . not clear! You just go and look at those

[1] Fields cleared from forest lands.

61

cleared lands. We used to harvest grain from those fields, and now nothing but logs."

Kirka is called up before the village Soviet. "Try and control the old man," they tell him. "You know what would have happened to you before for such speeches?"

"You're right, comrades. . . . Your observation's true," Kirka agrees. "The old man's going too far. Only I can't contradict my father. I wasn't brought up that way. You'll also take that into account, comrades."

There was much talk in the village about the new Pozdeyev house. The villagers not only talked, but every one on foot or on horseback used to stop nearby. The house had been built in a new way, in the city manner: a kitchen, a bedroom for Kirka and his wife, a room for the old couple, and a nursery. Kirka, according to his own words, had also planned to have seven sons during the seven-year-plan period; and, you have to hand it to him, he kept up with the plan, for his wife was always walking around with a big belly.

The Pozdeyev house had another curious feature. The little garret, or attic, as they call it locally, was no mere chicken coop under the roof (these attics are not so rare now in the new houses), but a real room with paneled walls, a couple of windows, and a little balcony.

As for this attic, to which Kirka had given priority and whose balcony rails he'd even found time to paint pale blue, the old man raved and protested against it: it was bad enough to have to put up such a queer structure, but to engage in such extra fancies as well, that was the limit. Before Anany Yegorovich even had time to enter, Ignat was shouting and pointing at the attic:

"Just look at what he's invented! He needs a little sky parlor. But who got the timber ready for him?" Turning abruptly to his son, the old man asked, his beard jerking up: "Was it you?"

Kirka, smiling condescendingly, shrugged his wide shoulders slightly and drove his axe to rest in a block.

They sat down, all of them, on a dry log under the lean-to.

"Have you felled a lot of trees?" Ignat demanded, an unexpected question as always.

Stumped, Anany Yegorovich asked him what kind he meant.

"What kind . . . what kind. . . . Wood, of course!" the old man creaked in reply. "So you go on dawdling around other people's houses?"

That Anany understood. The old man was hinting it was time, so to speak, for him, Anany, to build a nest of his own, if he wished them to take any notice of him as a kolhoz chairman.

But Ignat did not wait for an answer—everybody is deaf in his own way—and shouted once more:

"And why are you holding on to your cheek? Are your teeth sore? Of course they should be sore! Who helped you think up this notion of switching people from the hay harvesting? Eh?"

"Stop shouting," Kirka suggested, vaguely adding: "The Party knows . . ."

"Look here, Pozdeyev, you'd better not talk about the Party."

"But, comrade chairman, I was just saying . . ." Kirka always addressed Anany Yegorovich by his official title. "I was referring to the Program. . . . I hear there'll be a seminar one of these days soon."

"There will be. But I advise you to keep your tongue in check. Don't dream of starting up a circus."

"What's that?" shouted Ignat.

"You have a good house, he says," Kirka lied without even a blink of his eyes.

"That's so, that's so," the old man nodded with satisfaction. "A good house. In the autumn we'll celebrate our housewarming. Will you come?"

Anany Yegorovich nodded and stood up: the decencies had been observed, and he hadn't time now for more idle chatter.

VIII. The Village In Construction

One evening when he had stayed late in the office with Isakov, the Party secretary, they counted up thirty-two new houses in the village. Thirty-two! And all these houses had been newly built within the last eight years.

"Can you imagine what this means?" asked Isakov significantly. "And just look inside one of these houses! You'll find a nickel-plated bed, a sewing machine, and the radio. And some of these people even have bicycles!" Isakov pondered for a while, then smiled. "I was in Zarechie not long ago. Do you know Prokhorov's house there? Very spacious, two stories, a regular mansion—the house at the upper end, remember? In 'thirty they had already dealt

with Prokhorov as a kulak. True, they rehabili-
tated him later. It didn't do any good to have
that peasant rotting in Solovki.[1] He'd accumu-
lated everything with the hump of his labor.
But in those days Prokhorov was a rich man all
right. Everyone envied him. 'Well, you don't
really mean that,' they'd say. 'How can you
compete with Prokhorov? He has a copper
hand basin instead of a wooden bowl.' Well, a
few days ago I dropped in to see his son. He
lives alone. His brothers were all killed off in
the war. 'Well, Andrey,' I said 'show me your
kulak way of living. What inheritance did your
father leave you?' Andrey just laughed. 'Look
around,' he said. Well, I looked. The copper
hand basin was under the tap—that's true
enough. And what else? A little black cupboard for the dishes—in those days the villagers
used to gossip a lot about that little cupboard
too: 'Look at the way the Prokhorovs live.
They got themselves a cupboard with glass
doors for their dishes.' Well, I looked at that
little cupboard. If you gave it away free now,
no one would take it. Well, and that's about
all." And Isakov concluded, "It means we're
not living so badly today. Things are changing,
even here with us in the North."

Yes, it was all like that. And if a historian

[1] Solovetskie Islands, in the White Sea, site of a Soviet
labor camp.

had questioned him, he, Anany Yegorovich, would have had plenty more to tell on the subject—the village was renewing itself under his eyes.

And it had all begun with the district center, with the state employees. A great many of all sorts of state employees had flocked to the district center after the war. Endless "district bodies" sitting in almost every house—very touchingly described in a certain book—were emptying the villages of anything with the slightest claim to literacy. And it was this layer of petty officialdom which, bored at having nothing to do after official hours (it was no joke for a healthy peasant to be idle after six o'clock!) began to indulge in a bit of sport with their axes. In this way, while the village was being emptied and was breaking up, new houses began to spring up like mushrooms in the district center. That's the way things were. And it was only after 'fifty-three that new roofs began to whiten the village landscape.

"All the same, twist and turn as you may," Anany Yegorovich said to himself, "there is one question you can't escape. Where does the wealth come from on which village life is built? The income from the kolhoz? No, not from there—that's the trouble! Who did all right for himself over these years? Those who got financial aid on the side. In some cases from pensions; in others maybe from a son in the timber industry; in others again, from a state employee in the family. Take those Pozdeyevs, for example. If Kirka's wife had not been a bookkeeper in the Co-op, he would never even have seen the house he was now building."

In the village it was now accepted that, if you worked in a kolhoz, you sought a wife who was state employed, so there would always be a kopeck in the house. After the war, at the time of the monetary reform, this procedure was even given a special name of its own— "to marry a round loaf." In a word, if you thought about it, a peculiar kind of family unit was in process of being formed—a family in which the economic factor was by no means negligible.

Among the new houses you came across there were quite a few that had their windows boarded up. A house seemed finished—you only needed to pull the boards down and start living in it. But these houses remained uninhabited.

The new houses with their boarded windows were like a stone in the kidney of every kolhoz chairman. As a rule they were owned by workers in the timber industry—the kolhoz workers of yesterday who, for good reasons or bad, had quit the kolhoz at some time. Well, so they had quit. Why shouldn't they live their own way? The forest settlements now had all the comforts, and the villages could not rival them. But come summer, and you began to notice now one man with an ax walking around the site of his former ancestral home, now another floating construction timber down the river, come spring and a third. . . .

What was this? Man's age-long attachment to his native soil, to the nest where he was born? Or had the peasant in him not yet been thoroughly aired out of him? A man got his leave of absence, and what did he do with it? Somehow he must kill time! Then wasn't it simpler for him to build his own house near his work—in a forest settlement? Or were those kolhoz workers of yesterday expecting some great change in village life?

Khudyukov turned out to be a worthless synoptic. True, the rain was gradually slowing down, but there was still no sun.

Anany Yegorovich turned aside toward a few other houses. But their gates were latched. Most likely, their inhabitants had also gone off into the forest for mushrooms. . . .

He heard the sound of an ax nearby. The sound died away, and then the thudding was renewed.

Turning the corner of an old hut, Anany Yegorovich saw the usual spectacle: the newly built framework of a house in a fenced-in field, and a man standing at one of its corners. It was Ivan Yakovlev—one of those former kolhoz workers who after the war had swelled the army of workers attached to the local Timber Industry Collective.

"Not afraid of getting soaked?" Anany Yegorovich asked, approaching the new structure.

"I don't mind. I'm not made of sugar."

"So, so. You're thinking of returning home then?"

"H'm," Ivan replied. "Maybe I will."

"Hurry up then. We'll take you in this very day."

"You'll take me in all right, I know. But what about this?" Ivan said, rubbing three of his fingers together. "Conditions here are kind of meager and poor. I manage to knock off a hundred—a hundred and fifty—rubles in the forest."

"Well, that depends entirely on us. Once we improve the kolhoz, we'll have a merrier time with the ruble."

"Then I'll wait a while, comrade Mysovsky. I'm in no hurry!"

The same old story. It was like a vicious circle! To make the daily labor norm attractive, people had to work. What other source of income was there for the kolhoz? But to get people to work, you had to have an attractive daily norm.

Where was the solution?

In the district committee they had told him, "You're giving bad leadership. You've soft-pedaled agitational and educational work." But how were you going to bring agitational pressure on the kolhoz worker of today? Without money, agitation didn't get you anywhere. You tried to argue like this: "We've bought two tractors, haven't we?" "Yes, we have!" "Do we need money for trucks?" "Sure we do." "And for the new barns for livestock? And haven't we set up a public radio system?" "You've got to wait a little. We'll improve the labor norm soon enough." But he, the kolhoz worker of today, refused to wait. He did not want to wait any longer. That's what the trouble was.

IX. The Survival

At first he thought it was a sunflower. So bright did it glow and shimmer among the green vegetables!

But he was mistaken. The bright patch in the orchard in front of the hut was no sunflower at all but a woman's traditional headdress or, to be precise, the round brocade top of a headdress. And it was no young girl who was thus adorned (the young, in general, no longer wear headdresses), but an old crone—small and withered. Bending over a vegetable bed and shaking her bright head slightly, she was tugging fiercely at the onions, evidently for her meal, for she was barefoot and had on a faded blue sarafan such as old women wear.

"Your good health, Tikhonovna," Anany Yegorovich exclaimed, approaching the orchard.

The old woman straightened her back energetically and winked slyly:

"You recognized me then. And there I was watching you secretly and thinking, 'He's getting above himself—will he pass by or stop to greet me?'"

"Well, it's not hard to recognize you. Look at the way you shine!"

"Keep quiet, for God's sake. Don't shame me. I know myself it's not right. I used to walk about in this headdress as a young girl. Then I kept it for my daughter, Marussia. But now that Marussia doesn't wear it, am I supposed to throw away a good thing? One man criticizes, another understands."

Agafya Tikhonovna, or Aganya Paleyá (as they called her in the village for her rare sprightliness) was very well known to almost all the state employees in the district. She was a most hospitable and convivial old woman. While you were drinking tea with her, she'd tell you everything: what the new chairman was like, how different people worked, and what, in her opinion, was not quite right in the kolhoz and how it should be corrected. And she would describe all of this in very picturesque language, spiced with jokes and pithy sayings. Officials on missions began to stay in her house as the occasion demanded, but that only in summer, for the old woman always spent winter with her daughter in town.

"Let's go inside," Tikhonovna suggested with characteristic hospitality as she came out of the orchard with a bunch of onions. "My samovar's already singing."

And why, indeed, shouldn't he have a quick bite of something? He didn't know when he would get home. Yes, maybe a little hot food would ease his toothache.

In her low, noticeably sagging cottage, it was warm, even hot. The floor was scrubbed with sand; the prominent knots on the wide, old deal boards gleamed like onions. Tikhonovna was always known for her tidiness.

Anany Yegorovich, feeling at home—everything here was familiar to him—took off his soaking raincape and spread it out on the joist of the stove. Let the raincape get warm too!

"Are your feet dry? Shall I give you a pair of felt boots?" Tikhonovna asked.

Perhaps that was superfluous. He'd stay only briefly. He hadn't time to sit about.

Tikhonovna, her bare feet shuffling, laid the table in a jiffy. Cod, town-baked hard rolls—this was obligatory when she had a visitor from town—soaked wild raspberries with granulated sugar, brown mushrooms with onion. And to round it off, a boiling samovar.

"Drink—eat, little guest," Tikhonovna said in the ancient manner and, not without playfulness, bowed low to the waist.

Then, with the top of her headdress gleaming, she, as the mistress of the house, took her seat by the samovar.

"It's not tea I should be giving you. Dear Guest! But grandma has no 'moonshine' left. My grandson, the day before yesterday, rolled in drunk: 'Grandma,' he says, 'give me vodka or I'll set you on fire.' 'What's this, you drunken mug,' says I to him, 'aren't you ashamed to talk to your grandma like that?' Then I gave him the vodka—the further from sin, the better."

Tikhonovna warmed up over tea. The sweat stood out in beads on her dark, wrinkled forehead, while her small, well-formed ears turned as pink as a young girl's.

"How old is she? The other side of eighty?" Anany Yegorovich asked himself. "A hard nut she is!" And Tikhonovna had a pair of pale blue eyes with a wily glint still sharp, and firm, not yet watery, pupils.

"Well, and how was your stay in town? Did you like it?" he inquired, breaking a hard roll.

"Did-not-plea-dse-me-at-all." Tikhonovna, evidently not loath to show off some of her newly acquired city words, enunciated these words assiduously accenting every syllable.

"Why so?"

"The young people did not plea-dse me at all," the old woman answered, again accentuating the "d."

"The young people?"

"The young people," Tikhonovna nodded affirmatively. She wiped her face with the dry palm of her hand. "We were walking along, my Marussia and I, through town. It was the time of the May holidays. The people just flowed—like water pouring. I gaped and forgot everything else. Then I suddenly stopped: where was my Marussia? Hither, thither—no Marussia. I ask one man, another—they just laughed: 'a crazy old woman.' And then, in a small garden, I see a girl standing up. She was standing high. On a little platform. She herself was all white, her head was bent, she had a tie on and was reading from a book. 'See here, girl,' I say, 'look around you. Can you see my Marussia anywhere?' The girl, she doesn't say a word. I tell her the same thing again: 'You're standing on a little platform,' I say, 'you can see everything. Will you look around you.' But the girl just won't speak. So I lost my patience: 'Shameless hussy,' I say, 'you're literate, you can read a book. Why do you find it so hard to talk—will your tongue fall out or what?' But just then Marussia came running. And she asks me with a grin: 'Whom are you talking

with, *babka*?' 'What do you mean, with whom?
I'm talking with . . . this . . . hussy.' 'What are
you doing, you silly *babka*? That girl isn't
alive.' "

Anany Yegorovich burst out laughing. How
is it he didn't guess at once that Tikhonovna
was leading him up the garden path? She had
always been a past master at all sorts of
fantasies.

And pausing for him to stop laughing, Tikhonovna concluded:

" 'Not alive?' I ask. 'How not alive?' I say.
'She's reading a book, and she has a tie on . . .'
'It's a stature,' says Marussia. 'A stature? And
why,' I asked, 'have they set up the statures?
Aren't there enough alive people in the town?' "

"So, so," Anany Yegorovich said, laughing
again. "You say you weren't pleased to be
in town? It's better here with us then?"

"And it doesn't plea-dse me here either."

"That's a blow!"

"The bosses here don't plea-dse me. You
don't plea-dse me," Tikhonovna insisted, suddenly sitting up straight and sternly compress-
ing her sunken toothless mouth. "What's
happening here? The hay's all going to rot.
The best quality hay too. This morning I was
coming from the forest with a good picking of
salting mushrooms. I look, and there's the
whole village up in smoke. Oi, I feel bad, it

must be a fire. No, it isn't a fire. It's our
bedridden ones just waking up and lighting
their stoves. My neighbor, that stripling of a
woman, comes rolling out on the porch, herself
more than the width of it, and starts scratching
her fat behind." Here Tikhonovna jumped up
quickly from her stool and demonstrated how
her neighbor did this.

Anany Yegorovich, trying to remember which
of the younger people lived nearby, asked:

"Whose young woman was it?"

"Whose? Have you forgotten? Dunka of the
Afanasievs. She lives next door."

"But that stripling of a woman, as you call
her, is well on in years."

"In what years?" Tikhonovna demanded,
really angry now. "Don't slap the paint on so
thick, Anany Yegorovich. We know. Well on in
years indeed. How old is she? Is she sixty? She
might be sixty two, but no more. When I myself was given in marriage, she was still in
her mother's belly. In the old days, she was a
front-line worker. Let me tell you this," Tikhonovna added, snuffling reflectively. "I was
walking along one day, and a bunch of women
was sitting by the management office. The sun
was turning to noon, and a crane was straining
on the other side of the river and crying in
a desperate voice: 'What are you up to, you
bitches without a conscience, get up! It's harvest

time! The grain's weeping in the fields, the hay
is drying up . . .' And they, the little lilies, just
sitting about—you couldn't budge them with a
stake. They sit there puffing—you can hear
them a mile away. I'm thinking it's a disease of
sorts—they do nothing but complain of illness
. . . No, it's no disease. They were just waiting
for a machine, and there's only two miles to
walk. A shameful lot, they are! And how did
we use to manage without a machine? My
Olexandrushko was growing up then—killed in
the war, he was later, and my man was having
a hard time at Yurov, some ten miles from
home. I'd pick up the boy in my arms, sling a
bag with the bread over my back, and go off at
a run. I'd run as if whipped. Then, having
worked the day, you'd find your way home
again. The boy would be all bitten by mosqui-
toes—his eyes closed. During the war they also
had a conscience. They didn't burn out,"
Tikhonovna expressed herself in the new
jargon. "Just you walk through the fresh lands
—the 'bunions' haven't yet gone from the fields.
They used 'to kolhoz' so hard, their shirts were
never dry from sweat. But now those lands
are all overgrown. The trees there stand so
tall you could cut them down for sleigh
runners."

Tikhonovna rubbed her eyes and then blew
her nose into the hem of her skirt.

"No, nowadays, you can't expect a good living," she said with conviction. "Too many of these 'ladies' popping up. See—even the sun's ashamed to look at the earth. It's turned away —for two weeks it hasn't shown itself."

She stopped talking, then sighed.

"I don't paint my daughter any better. She's seen too much in town. 'Mashka, what are you lying in bed for? People are off to work already.' It's the disease, according to her. All my life, I haven't heard of the like—pertonia, it's called."

"Hypertonia," Anany Yegorovich corrected her.

"Well, well, I can't pronounce it. Not ours evidently, this disease, must be a foreign import. . . . Time passes, the pertonia's at an end, but my Marussia's back in bed again. 'What now, girl? A new *Dekhree!* The state must pay money—we don't bear children free . . .'"

Anany Yegorovich glanced at his watch. It was near six. Once Tikhonovna started talking there was no end to it.

"All right, I'll be going now," he said, getting up.

"Go, go. I told you everything straight in the eye. Like it, or not—you must listen. Well, they don't expect much of me—I'm just a survival."

Anany Yegorovich glanced questioningly at the old woman.

"A survival, yes, a survival," she nodded her head. "That's so. That's what they've called us old women all our lives. If one doesn't displease the likes of your fraternity—the authorities, I mean—then they start penalizing you for being a survival! Why, even my own blood, my own daughter, deigns to call me that: 'Hold your tongue,' she'll say, 'you old survival . . .'"

While he had been sitting inside Tikhonovna's cottage it had grown lighter in the street. The rain had stopped. Maybe Khudyakov was right after all—the weather would break. Steam was rising from his limp, stove-warmed raincape.

"Don't catch cold," Tikhonovna counseled him. "To look at you, you've gone all up in smoke like after a steam bath."

As with winter crops, her patch of land was thickly grown over with lush grass. The narrow path through it was barely visible—obviously the old woman had very few visitors.

As he came out on the road, Anany Yegorovich turned around once more. Tikhonovna stood barefoot on the steps and very lightly, like a sunflower, nodded her head surmounted with the bright-topped headdress.

A monument should be erected to these survivals!

X. The Old Communist

The house of a state employee or, as they say in the village, a "money man," can be distinguished immediately. It's more dressy, this house. Unfailingly, the window and door casings are painted; instead of a fence of simple stakes, an enclosure of lathe or a wattle of pine or fir. And, of course, a radio antenna on the roof (a public radio system had been set up in the kolhoz only the previous year).

Serafim Ivanovich Yakovlev was the chairman of the local Forest Chemical Association, and his house had yet another peculiarity—the front corners of the house, closely fixed with thin boards, were painted a solid dark green.

Serafim Ivanovich was home. He ran out

on the front steps, wearing a white shirt with an open collar next to his skin and a pair of galoshes on his bare feet.

"Come in a minute. I've business with you."

"And I have business with you too," replied Anany Yegorovich.

In the bright passage with large and small wooden tubs and buckets along the walls, there were three doors: the one straight ahead led into the kitchen; the other on the left, to the cow in the cowshed; and the third one to the right, nailed with black padding, as in a well-established institution of at least district rank, gave on one of the rooms.

Serafim Ivanovich pulled open just this padded door. The room—you could see this at a glance—was destined for very important guests. The high nickel-plated bed with a pile of white pillows under a muslin cover and a lacquered picture hanging on the wall depicting a bouncing beauty embracing a swan; tulle curtains the full height of the window; fig trees in tubs reaching out to the ceiling; and in the holy red corner, a whatnot with several books of party literature.

The mistress of the house, a thin sickly woman with the countenance of the Mother of God, noiselessly entered the room, placed a bottle of vodka and a plate with pickles on the table, and as noiselessly departed.

Serafim Ivanovich himself looked hale and hearty despite the fact that he was well over fifty (he was about four years older than Anany Yegorovich). His face was smooth, pink, and clean-shaven. There was not a touch of gray in his reddish bristling hair, which had not yet dried after his bath. And there was strength also in his close-set teeth, protruding like those of a horse.

"You shouldn't have done that, Yakovlev," said Anany Yegorovich, nodding at the bottle. "I haven't come for that."

"Who says you came for that? But since you're here, a little tumbler won't harm you. And maybe you'd like a steam bath? My little bathhouse is a beauty. There's as much water and heat as you like."

Anany Yegorovich, protesting he was too busy, came to the point:

"This is what I've come about. They tell me you're going on leave."

"Yes, I am. As of tomorrow. Here, let me pour you a drop," Serafim Ivanovich said and, winking convivially with his reddish eye, pushed a glass of vodka toward him.

Anany Yegorovich's teeth were still a bit sore. And a tumbler of vodka would not have been amiss. But he said to himself: "No, this isn't the time. People are already looking askance at me (the chairman is to blame for everything), and they might smell 'the perfume.' 'Ah,' they'd say, 'there's a fine goose for you. Keeps telling us what to do, but he's been steamed up himself since early morning.' "

"So you won't?"

"No, I won't."

"Well, as you like, but I'll drink." And Serafim Ivanovich, growing noticeably gloomier, emptied his tumbler in one gulp.

"How are you planning your day tomorrow? We're in an awful mess with the silage. We've decided to declare it a Work Sunday."

Serafim Ivanovich downed another glass.

"You can do it," he said, crunching a pickle.

Anany Yegorovich felt his heart grow lighter. He got up:

"Till morning then. We'll charge uphill."

"We can do that, we can," Serafim Ivanovich assented. "But I have a little request to make of you too. Will you scribble a certificate of leave for my boy?"

"For a certificate of leave you should apply to the management office," Anany Yegorovich replied dryly. "It decides."

"Well, you can tell that to others. I manage an office myself."

"An interesting point. Leave of absence for your son, leave of absence for someone else, and who is left to work in the kolhoz?"

"I think," said Serafim Ivanovich, enunciating every word very distinctly, "I think you ought to oblige me. I've been a party member since 'twenty-nine—are there many others like me in the village? Haven't I the right to educate one of my sons? You know yourself that, in these times, education is the very foundation of life."

Was it worth pursuing the subject? No, you couldn't produce an effect on a man like Yakovlev with mere words. He had, you see, rendered special services. . . . He, you see, was an old party member. And now it was for the Soviet power to serve him rather than for him to serve the Soviet power.

In any case, Anany Yegorovich, as he grasped the door handle, reminded him once more:

"We're agreed then? You'll turn up tomorrow."

"I will."

"He won't turn up," Anany Yegorovich decided.

He was seething inwardly. In the district committee they figured there were twenty-five communists in the kolhoz "New Life." A mighty nucleus. Yes, mighty on paper. But in reality? There were nine to ten pensioners, seven teachers, the chairman of the Village Soviet, its secretary, the forest ranger, the chairman of the Village Purchasing Organization and his bookkeeper, the Chairman of

Forest Chemical Association. . . . But which
of them was directly involved in kolhoz pro-
duction? Who lived and was nourished by it?
It was all mere appearance, the same sort of
window dressing. The party organization would
put through a decision. A right decision. But
who executed it? Always the same chairman
and two or three of the brigadiers. But the
rest of them remained spectators. They pursued
their own objectives. And so it came about
that they only acted as counselors, as con-
sultants of a sort, in the party organization.
No, when Isakov arrived from the district
center (he'd been summoned to the district
committee to report on visual instruction—he
couldn't have picked a better time!), he, Anany
Yegorovich would immediately face him with
this problem. They could not go on like this.

XI. *Petunya Bulldozer*

Should he call on Petunya Devyatyi?

Devyatyi's homestead was off the beaten track, beyond the village, by the grazing lands, and in order to get there you had to go down the hill and cross a stream.

Anany Yegorovich gazed at the road which was all broken up, rutted, and soggy with red clay, and listened to the purring brook under the hill. Maybe it wasn't worth his while to slosh all the way through this mud.

Petunya, according to the kolhoz files, was now unfit for labor. This winter he had reached his sixty-seventh year, and Anany Yegorovich recalled some talk of this in the office. But on the other hand, didn't everyone know that there was no man in the village who could match him in strength? It was not for nothing he'd been nicknamed Petunya Bulldozer! For example, when they were unloading a barge the previous fall, Petunya carried two sacks of flour at a time (to earn more!)—this Anany Yegorovich had seen with his own eyes. He had also seen Petunya in the meadows dealing with a load of hay. His co-worker, a young peasant, moved this way and that near the hayrick; dripping with sweat, he panted like a hard-ridden horse, while Petunya showed no undue haste: now he'd glance up at the sun, now he'd sniff at the hay, then take his measure again of the hayrick with his pitchfork as he approached from this side and that. Then you'd suddenly notice: the shock had been yanked from the ground and set on top of the hayrick.

"Where do you get all that strength, Pyotr Nikitich?" Anany Yegorovich had asked.

"Strength, you say? I must be of that breed. Besides, we Devyatyis, we don't drink tea."

"And is tea harmful to your strength?"

"It's a dissolvant. With water the strength goes out of a man."

Devyatyi had another quirk: he had to have his rest once a week. There was nothing you could do to get Petunya to budge! True, in the kolhoz this was taken into account—after all, on ordinary days Petunya did the work of four. But when he found himself in the timber camps soon after the war they treated him more roughly: he was tried for not turning up for work during a "shock work" month. But after they released him from the labor camps, Petunya still stuck to his guns.

"And aren't you afraid, Nikitich, that they'll shove you in again?" the peasants needled him.

"No, boys, I'm not afraid. The working class is resting, and is right in doing so. It increases productivity."

That was Petunya Bulldozer!

In late fall a year and a half ago—the very first year of Anany Yegorovich's management—Petunya appeared in the office and declared:

"That's how it is, comrades. I've overstrained myself. I don't want the brigadier to wear out his boots in vain," he said, presenting a medical certificate signed by the district doctor. This read: "Citizen Devyatyi, P.N., is suffering from chronic rheumatism in the joints of his lower extremities. He is in need of systematic treatment . . ."

This seemed in order.

But now, as he approached Devyatyi's homestead, Anany Yegorovich only shook his head: "Lord! What couldn't he do, this old man with rheumatic legs! And he had done all that in just a year and a half!"

The house had been newly roofed; in the

rear were a new bathhouse and ice-cellar; the enclosure of the homestead was also quite new, and the gates, freshly painted brown, hung on solid posts.

Where did Petunya's abundance come from? He received no pension, had no kopecks coming in on the side; he'd lived a whole age without any children, all alone with his old woman. Could his private homestead plot be the source of it all? Yes, it had already come to Anany Yegorovich's ears that Devyatyi had been doing a bit of private trading with the timber stations and had made a tidy little profit, but he had not paid much attention to the gossip. There was always a lot of talk in the village. But as he looked at this homestead he realized that people had not talked idly.

Petunya subordinated everything to the demands of the market. Instead of a small vegetable bed planted with onions, as is the custom in every other house, Petunya had a regular onion plantation. And the onions were first class—far superior to those of the kolhoz: the onion shoots—blue and juicy—were sprouting all over the vegetable beds like lush sedge, and the onion bulbs were as succulent and resistant as turnips. Beyond the onion beds were cucumbers under glass—a vegetable also in great demand but not yet properly exploited by the kolhozes in these parts. Then there was a long patch of potatoes. And that was all. There was no strip of rye or barley, no little patch of vetch mixed with oats, such as you would see in other kolhoz farmsteads.

And there was something else which attracted Anany Yegorovich's attention. Petunya had literally planted every inch of his ground. He had moved his woodshed and bathhouse to the other side of the fence, behind the house. And even the path leading from the wicket to the gate, which split the onion beds in two, had been so reduced that a cart could no longer pass there.

"Yes," Anany Yegorovich thought without joy, "so that's what the old devil's been up to. All by dint of hard toil. In some two or one and a half years. And he manages to live without applying for any public assistance. As for us. . . . For the last fifteen years we've been trying hard to raise the level of the kolhoz . . ."

Brusquely he wrenched the damp, still sodden wicket toward him; and at the same time he heard the house gates creak. The master of the house came out on the steps—a hard, sturdy old man, capless, his head cropped closely, wearing a short sheepskin coat slung over his shoulders and a pair of low felt boots.

"I'm not coming down to meet the guest. The hinges of my legs are too rusty," he declared from the eminence.

From the open passage a small shaggy dog of varied colors leaped out barking and dashed under the feet of Anany Yegorovich as he mounted the steps.

"Zhulka, get out," Petunya cried halfheartedly. "Run away."

The little dog stopped barking, wagged its tail, and began to sniff at Anany Yegorovich's feet.

"She's a little nothing. We keep her for pleasure," Petunya explained with a condescending nod toward the dog. "Will you come into the hut or are you in a hurry?"

"In a hurry."

"Well, you know best. But I'll sit down." And Petunya, holding onto the jambs of the doorway, lowered himself heavily on the steps. "Nowadays, in the damp, it's only the ants that save me. My old woman's gone out again prospecting for ant heaps."

"Doesn't the onion help?"

"What? Onion? No, it doesn't help. And I dislike it, too, that onion. And my old woman doesn't eat much either. It's just grass," the old man added skeptically.

"And I thought you were such a great lover

96

of green vegetables. You have whole planta-
tions over there!"

"No, that's not for myself. We grow vegetables for sale," Petunya replied again with
good-natured frankness.

Anany Yegorovich was beginning to lose
patience.

"And your conscience—it doesn't bother you?
You don't find it hard then to engage in trade
at your age?"

"It is hard. It's hard getting a horse. D'you
see the abundance of green shoots? But ask the
brigadier a thousand times to help you out, and
he won't come without a bottle."

"And you feed him liquor?"

"Yes, I do feed him that. At first I did my
bartering on the ration lines, but nowadays it's
from the hoof. It comes expensive," Petunya
said with a sigh.

"Now look here, comrade Devyatyi! You'd
better shut down pretty soon or, if you don't,
we'll shut your shop for you."

"You won't shut it," Petunya contradicted
him calmly.

"We will shut it. And how! Why, do you
think we'll stand there watching a private indi-
vidual operate under a kolhoz roof? If you
haven't got a conscience yourself, we'll find the
means."

Petunya was silent for a moment.

"You keep bringing up the conscience . . ." Petunya began, then paused again, rubbing his knees which were now at a right angle. Then he suddenly smiled: "This is what should be done in the matter of conscience, chairman. Here, in a certain kolhoz, lived an old man and his old wife. They were childless. Well, the old man had an accident—he fell ill, that is. His old woman naturally shed tears: 'How are we going to live? There isn't a kopeck in the house.' 'Never mind,' the old man answered, 'we'll manage. We've got no money, but we have a lot of conscience. How much of this conscience,' he says, 'have we both earned in the past twenty-nine years? Go,' he says, 'to the barn and fill a sack and try the shop . . .'"

"Perhaps we'd better postpone this tale?" Anany Yegorovich interrupted less heatedly.

"No, you'd better hear me out," Petunya insisted. "It's no invented tale. . . . Well, so the woman put the sack of conscience on her back and tried the shop. In an hour she was back. Weeping, she said, 'They won't accept our conscience. They only take cash.' 'Then,' said the old man, 'go to the kolhoz. They distribute conscience there. They'll give you goods in exchange.' But they wouldn't barter there either . . ."

Nothing was left to Anany Yegorovich but

to swallow Petunya's sermon in silence. To what could he object? What would he himself have done in the old man's place? And, to be frank, he'd even taken a liking to this old man. He liked him for his sincerity and forthrightness.

Petunya made no attempt to dodge the issue of tomorrow's Work Sunday.

"No, don't count on me," he said. "If I had a little cow, maybe I'd have made the effort. But I've no little cow. . . . And who wants to break his back?"

Again the cow question! And this in a kolhoz which was literally smothered with pasture. Every year, dozens, hundreds, and, if you counted all the streams, thousands of acres even, were under snow, and yet a good half of the kolhoz workers owned no cow. Wasn't that fantastic? But the explanation was very simple. Ten percent of all the harvested kolhoz hay was all that a worker received as his daily labor norm. What did that mean? It meant that the kolhoz worker, in order to earn enough to buy a cow, must furnish sufficient hay for at least eight or nine cows (two tons of hay according to the statistics)—something absolutely unthinkable even if the technical means were adequate.

Did the kolhozes understand this? Sure they understood it. And each chairman, in one way or another, tried to get around this system. But at this point the district prosecutor or the secretary of the district committee would intervene and threaten: "Don't you dare! It's an anti-government practice! The encouragement of private enterprise . . ."

So the "state" practice triumphs: in the autumn still another section of the kolhoz workers is deprived of its "wet nurse" (it's no village life without a cow!); in the springtime there is a further decline in livestock because fodder is short; and every year it becomes more difficult to find people for the hay harvest . . .

It was twilight. . . . At last the wind had dissipated the moist blanket; and outside the village the sunset spread a red strip on the fringe of the forest. For the first time in many days.

Anany Yegorovich walked wearily along the street curb, and his thoughts were far from joyous. He had walked through about a third of the village, had visited almost every house, had talked incessantly trying to persuade, convince, and shame them. . . . And what had he achieved? Would the people go out into the fields tomorrow to work on the silage?

At that hour the village was leading its customary life. The housewives darted about their grass patches, flashing their pale ankles—

some carrying buckets, some carrying greens; the cows mooed from time to time; axes thudded on the new construction sites. It would be a long time now, not till darkness fell, before this evening interchange between the axes would die away; and through the puddles, brimmed with red light, splashed barefoot urchins—looking pale and faded from the long days of rain as from some infirmity.

And the smells were the same as they had been five and thirty years ago. The smell of hot milk and irritating bathhouse smoke, mingled with that of birch brooms.

XII. And Still Another Question

There is nothing worse than to drop by a house in the middle of a family row or, as they like to say nowadays (people have become very cultured!), an "instructional ten minutes." It was at that very moment, during these instructional ten minutes, that Anany Yegorovich arrived at the Voronitzins. "You drunken mug," "you spigot," "you parasite"—all these familiar epithets, and many others even stronger, with which Polina was belaboring her husband, reached Anany's ears as he entered the house.

But Anany Yegorovich had no time to attend to the domestic drama (it was easy to understand why Polina was making it hot for her husband), and so he came right to the point—construction work.

Pavel Voronitzin said not a word. He sat at the table, his shoulders hunched, his stubby fingers spread out on his knees; he wore a sweater, a pair of soiled boots, and stared with gloomy detachment at a floor thick with cigarette butts and spit. The dim glimmer of a lamp set on an overturned earthenware pot cut slantingly across his red, fleshy face.

"Why the devil are you so silent? Who am I talking to? The walls?"

Pavel slowly raised his head, glanced silently at his wife, and then lowered it again.

In the shadow by the curtain Polina's eyes flashed sharply, like a cat's.

"It's always the same. He'll drink himself stupid, the devil, and just sit there—you can't squeeze a word out of him."

Anany Yegorovich sat down at the table.

"Look here, Voronitzin. Stop this idle nonsense. I ask you in all good faith: do you realize what will happen to the cows if your brigade doesn't come through on the construction job?"

"With the cows? Ekh, you . . ." Voronitzin suddenly sat up and sent a wave of alcoholic breath into the chairman's face. "But if I don't feel human, what then?"

"You ought to ease up on the vodka, then

you'd feel more human," Polina interjected.

"Just a moment, Polina Arkhipovna," Anany intervened, and then turned to Voronitzin. "What do you mean—you 'don't feel human'?"

"Just that. Do you have a passport?"[1]

"Yes, I have."

"But I haven't got one. I'm like a kolhoz ram walking around without a passport."

"I don't quite get you," Anany Yegorovich said after a pause.

"You don't get me?" Voronitzin asked with a crooked smile. "Sure you don't! Do you remember I went to town this spring? Remember? To fetch some spare parts?"

"Well, yes, I do."

"And you wrote out a kolhoz reference for me? In it you said I could draw some money on account! A leap-year sort of reference that was! I went to the teller at the Savings Bank and shoved this here reference in at the teller's window. And there was a female teller, all painted up and curled from head to toe. And she sniggered back at me: 'This is no identity card!' So I had to make the rounds, go to the regional executive committee, from one floor to another, from one desk to another—for two whole days I tried to prove that I was no swindler but a man." Voronitzin, again exhaling

[1] A form of identity card required for internal travel and for city dwellers.

a breath of raw liquor, abruptly moved closer to Anany Yegorovich. "Why haven't I got a passport?" he demanded. "Without one, I'm not a person, am I?"

"Well, Pavel Ivanovich, you've got to realize you're not the only one in that position. No kolhoz workers have passports."

"And why don't they have them?"

"Because the passport system has not been applied to the countryside."

"And why hasn't it been applied?"

"Why? Why? You're repeating yourself like a child. What do you need a passport for, anyway?"

"Because I need it. . . . Is that clear?"

Anany Yegorovich now began explaining in an official tone:

"We issue a passport, comrade Voronitzin, when a man is leaving a kolhoz. But you, I hope, have no intention of departing?"

"But if I should want to?"

Here Polina came to Anany Yegorovich's assistance.

"Where would you go, you ugly mug? You'll have to work anyway, wherever you are. You won't get anything free anywhere."

"Polina, don't interfere!" Voronitzin shouted, his face twitching. But he immediately regained control of himself. "But suppose I want to go?"

Anany Yegorovich waded in:

"All right. Put in an application. If the kolhoz management gives you the document you can do as you please—go to the North Pole if you wish!"

"But if I don't get one?" Voronitzin kept asking with drunken obstinacy.

"What evil spirits are you chasing with your passport?" Polina shouted, in a fury. "You're wound up: passport! passport! You'd lose it anyway the next time you got drunk. And you'd have to pay a ten-ruble fine! As it is, you keep losing lots of things, don't you?"

"Polina, stop talking!"

"Don't spin all these stupid yarns, then I'll stop talking. You just wait—they'll pinch your tongue. You've really burst the dam. You fill up till your eyes bulge, and then shoot your mouth off. The cottage is full of children—you should be working, not gabbing."

Voronitzin stopped gabbing. He looked at his wife with a long stare and then said with a sigh:

"Ekh you! Cattle-breeder . . ."

XIII.

It was Saturday, and the usual sight awaited him at home: the children were asleep after a steam bath and Lydia, full of energy, was sitting at a table with a lamp on it.

Lydia was, of course, embroidering. Embroidering the current cat or stag, images of which were already displayed on all the walls.

Anany Yegorovich took off his raincape and put on a pair of warm felt boots. Lydia did not utter a word; she did not even glance in his direction. Well, she was right in her own way: the bathhouse had been heated for him too. Trying to relieve his guilt, he approached her from the side and placed a hand of reconciliation on her warm, full shoulder.

Lydia stood up without a word and began to lay the table.

He prodded the dry potatoes with his fork, prodded the mushrooms and, with a sigh, pushed the plate aside.

"Ah, you turn up your nose again! You don't like it? And what about the children?"

And so she went on. What sort of a chairman are you, when you can't even get milk in the kolhoz? Whoever heard of having no milk in a kolhoz! We have to pay kolhoz people thirty kopecks a quart. Who will ever respect you after this?

And he had to explain to her for the umpteenth time: yes, there was no milk in the kolhoz! The plan had not been fulfilled! The nursery school was on a starvation diet! Even the teachers are not given milk! How is it she can't understand this?

But as far as Lydia was concerned it was like water off a duck's back. And once she'd taken the bit between her teeth you couldn't stop her.

"So why the devil did you ever bring us here?" she demanded, as always playing her last ace. "How often have I said to you: 'Anany, we must not go there.' 'Anany, don't try to act the youngster! People in their sixties should be thinking of their pension, and you—

there's a young hero!—go off to raise the level of a kolhoz.'"

"Enough!" Anany Yegorovich shouted, brusquely leaving his chair. "You've got used to living like a lady. The wife of the deputy chairman of the Regional Executive Committee! The regional aristocracy. . . . No, you'd better shovel manure with the peasant women. . . ."

Petka, their youngest son, awoke and gazed from his bed with a frown at his parents.

Anany Yegorovich made a hopeless gesture with his hand what else could he do?—and went into another room. So that was the heart-to-heart talk he'd been having with his wife! The way she'd welcomed him, her husband, and comforted him! His nerves had been racked enough that day, but there'd been still more to come—he'd had another portion at home.

Without undressing he lay down in his jacket and stretched his legs. Oh, if he could only doze off for a while! If he could only forget himself for ten minutes. . . .

He could hear her heavy steps, the rattle of plates in the other half of the apartment. Then everything quieted down, and in the dry, resonant silence he detected the familiar click of a needle.

He stared through the open door. As he expected. Lydia was sitting at the embroidery frame. Cold and unapproachable. With a smooth, heavy head of hair, furrowed by a white parting.

He compressed his lips. Was that, indeed, Lydia? Was that really the same Lydochka, the young secretary to the Village Soviet who had been ready to go through fire and water with him?

In 'thirty, Anany Mysovsky, a recently demobilized Red Army man, was sent "to collectivize" in the R. . . district. The Village Soviet that fell to his lot was a distant and remote one. While traveling there by peasant sledge, he had almost frozen stiff—such was the horrific frost that year. But still he flew into the Village Soviet like an eagle—in a long cavalryman's coat and a Red Army helmet.

"Is it about the kolhozes you've come, comrade?" asked the black-eyed, pink-cheeked girl who met him at the door.

"No, it's about marriage," Anany had answered, laughing. (At the time he had pale, finely shaped lips, and he was fond of laughing.)

"Who's your bride then?" the girl asked, smiling in her turn.

"Who? Yourself, if you like. Agreed?"

The girl was not put out.

"Agreed," she said with challenge in her eyes.

The joke took a serious turn. Within three days they were man and wife. That was what Lydia had been like.

But now. . . . There she would be sitting in front of you, a heavy, stupid female, with her nose glued to that damned embroidery frame just like a horse to a bag of oats, and she did not seem to care about anything else even if a fire were raging all around them. . . .

He put his hand over his face. What had happened? How had it all come about? The years claimed their own. Ah, those years, those years. . . . Yes, in that year of 'thirty, he knew how to marry on the run, and much else besides. Just you try and turn a whole village upside down in a couple of days! And they *had* turned it upside down. Turned it upside down, the two of them! He a young man of twenty-three, a mere boy by present standards, and the chairman of that Village Soviet, a half-literate, former red partisan. They had turned the village upside down. Because the district committee had laid it down—either make a thorough job of it in two days or turn in your party cards. . . .

Anany Yegorovich lit a cigarette. On the stool nearby stood a lamp as always, and there was a newspaper too (Lydia still catered to his habits). He lit the lamp and, still lying on his back, unfurled the paper. "The Regional Football Championship." "Workers' Leave In Danger Of Being Canceled."

He turned over the page. That was not it, not for him. But here was something that concerned him. "News From The Front Line." "The First Testament Of The Kolhoz Workers." "Yes," thought Anany Yegorovich, "it's seventeen years since the end of the second world war, but we are still fighting on the agricultural front. We have to battle for every forty pounds of grain. . . . The news from the front line was not consoling. Rain, machines held up, absenteeism among the kolhoz workers. . . .

He put aside the paper and pondered. No, it had been easier in 'thirty. They'd been able to turn a whole village upside down. In two days! . . . "Maybe it was all so difficult now because it had been so easy then!" the thought suddenly occurred to him. How had the chairman of that Village Soviet and himself created the kolhoz then? "Why don't you enroll? Don't you like the Soviet authorities? Are you trying to help the enemy? . . ." Yes, that was the way they had recruited the peasants then. . . .

Anany Yegorovich rose abruptly. He was in a mess with his fodder, his hay was rotting, and what the devil was he thinking about!

When he came out into the front room and began to change his boots, Lydia frowned but said nothing. She had grown accustomed to his going out in the evening.

XIV.

There was nobody in the office, of course. It was an August darkness and the streets were empty. Only high above, on the posts, radio loudspeakers raged like machine guns through the village.

A light flickered on a slope near a shop. Probably it was the saleswoman or the night watchman. Yes, how good it would be to buy a half-bottle, return home to the warm cottage, and take a sip of vodka with his tea. It would be good, indeed, especially since his teeth had begun aching again.

Trudging through the puddles in the dark, Anany Yegorovich took the direction of the club. If a film was showing that night, he'd be certain to see one of the brigadiers.

The club was another sore tooth in the kolhoz. There had been a time when the problem of the club had been easily settled: with ropes and to shouts of "hurrah!" they had pulled down the crosses from the churches, adapted the altar to make a stage—and there was the club. And you had to admit that this kolhoz had had no problems with the club in the past twenty years. But the old church was now on its last legs—they'd had to shore up the ceiling twice. They would have to put up a new building. And, Anany said to himself, they'd have to do it if only to keep the young people in the kolhoz. A full day's work wasn't enough for the young. They wanted pleasure too.

They were dancing in the club. Around the thick, roughly planed beams supporting the high dark vaults, the younger fry swarmed like gnats in a forest, while the older girls—senior school girls, students on holiday, and milkmaids—were circling in the middle of the floor.

Anany Yegorovich stopped in the half-dark of the open doorway. He could see no men. The village swains today are mostly callow, adolescent schoolboys; and, if by chance some demobilized soldier appeared in the village, he would literally be beseiged on all sides, for there was an overproduction of potential brides in the kolhoz.

One dance ended, another began.

Three youths, all the "solid" variety—they were students—leaped to the side of Nyura Yakovleva. Nyura shrugged her shoulders coquettishly. "What shall I do with you all?" she asked. Then she smiled at one, smiled at another, and gave her hand to the third, a tall, fair-haired youth, the son of the woman teacher.

"Well, that one won't stay unmarried very long," Anany Yegorovich thought. "Looks as if we'll really have to find a new milkmaid soon." Then, looking at the young ones trampling the floor on one spot—in his day, they used to dance in a different way, with more vim—he noticed Elsa, the milkmaid brigadier. Elsa sat alone in a corner by the stove—a place usually occupied by girls no longer young who were not competing in the marriage lottery. The light of a wall lamp fell on her from above, and there was something pitiful, dreary, and sacrificial about her hunched up figure. . . .

Unexpectedly, Klavdia Nekhoroshkova appeared in the doorway. Tall, erect as a pole, her boots spattered with mud, the hem of her dress soaking—she must have arrived straight from Zarechie. Klavdia was tight. Her face was as flushed as a muzhik's, and her bright eyes

119

had a feverish gleam. For a while she stood immobile in the doorway scrutinizing the dancers, then she suddenly blurted out for the whole club to hear:

"Shurka! What the fuck are you playing there? Give us the old Russian dance tune!"

The dancers smiled as they glanced at her.

"Shurka! Do you hear me?" she called out, stamping her feet and shuffling noisily.

Shurka, an undersized schoolboy accordionist, glanced sideways at Danila, the village librarian who, tapping the floor with the metal end of a stick, was already approaching Klavdia.

"Dance if you want, but the street's the place for swearing and spitting," he said.

"What? You're giving me instructions, are you! Get out of here, you. . . ."

Anany Yegorovich squeezed Klavdia's elbow with some force.

"Stop it, Nekhoroshkova!"

"Ah, the chairman! . . . It was you I was looking for. Will you pay the price of a small bottle. . . ."

There was laughter in the hall.

"It's not a small bottle you need, but your brains examined. You're drunk, and in public."

"In public?" Klavdia stopped laughing. "The public beat it into the forest this morning. Well, I'll make them dance. They tried to cheat *me,* Klavdia!" she suddenly cried out, frowning at the silenced hall. "In the morning, I'll drag them all out. God be my witness. By the scruff of the neck!"

"You will, you will, you'll drag them out," said Anisia Yermolina, the mother of twin girls, appearing from nowhere and breaking into the conversation. "But you shouldn't spoil the young people's fun," she tried to persuade Klavdia. "Look at the little darlings there, how quiet they've become, their eyes fixed on the floor for shame. How can you use such expressions in front of young girls?"

"I'm a young girl myself!" Klavdia announced loudly with a smile. And then, to the accompaniment of laughter and cries, she grabbed the fat, awkward Anisia and dragged her off into the middle of the hall.

Shurka started to play the traditional Russian dance.

Anisia tried to free herself and they both fell down.

"Leave me alone!" Anisia shouted, scrambling up. "You keep to yourself, and I'll keep to myself. I'm the mother of virgins! I can't be seen with my bottom up!"

There was a new outburst of laughter and squealing. The performance would not be over very soon.

Anany Yegorovich walked out. It was useless

talking to Klavdia now. She was just pig-headed until she'd shake off her drunken folly.

It was amazing all the same, he thought, how people change. He had known Klavdia for a long time, a very long time, ever since the war years. He recalled arriving once at a hay harvest—in those days the district commit-tee agents stuck close to the kolhozes: it was a difficult period—the Soviet armies were in re-treat on all fronts. And here were these women sitting about the meadow and discussing for all they were worth, giving their souls free rein. But to one side, in the bushes, stood a slender girl with drooping head.

"Our brigadier," explained the women laugh-ingly. "We've sent her into the bushes. 'Go off with you, Klavka, while we'll talk real Russian a while—we'll feel the better for it.'"

Yes, that's how he'd seen Klavdia for the first time.

And he also remembered the following inci-dent. In 'forty-seven he, as the deputy of the chairman of the district executive committee, had arrived at the kolhoz for a report session. He had arrived with glad news: the District Consumers Union had set aside for the kolhoz workers forty yards of satin and five women's kerchiefs. The report was, of course, immedi-ately pushed aside, and the distribution of cloth headed the agenda for the day. Their clothes had worn down terribly—not a single yard of cloth had reached the village during all the war years.

Not without some bickering the satin was apportioned between the widows and the orphans. The kolhoz chairman suggested that the kerchiefs—cheap white kerchiefs with printed flowers—should be given to the younger girls.

They began calling out names again.

"For Klavdia Nekhoroshkova," someone proposed.

"She can wait!" various voices were heard. "She's in no hurry. Those who're still young should be the first to get them."

So Klavdia did not get her kerchief.

Anany Yegorovich, remembering this incident of long ago, suddenly understood the whole of Klavdia's senseless, broken life. Too old—make way! And what is a person to do who is "too old"? Was Klavdia to blame that her youth had been swallowed in the war? So she had started making her evening sorties into the village—maybe a crumb of female happiness would fall her way, and to hide the shame of it she'd drown her eyes in vodka. . . .

The weather was clearing. Large August stars were shining in the sky, and now one could distinguish the puddles on the roads.

"Why am I so sorry for everyone today?" Suddenly Anany Yegorovich was angry with himself. "Am I a kolhoz chairman or the manager of an almshouse? No, the devil take it all! Pity one, pity another, and who'll do the hard work?"

There was another place where men went on Saturdays—the tearoom. And he set off for the tearoom.

XV.

It was light in the room. Sunshine too. A lot of sunshine.

Had he not dreamed this? He passed the palm of his hand over his face. His palm was moist.

"Lydia!"

No answer.

He jumped out of bed and ran into the other rooms in his underwear.

No one there. On the table a note: "I've gone to the forest with the children."

He glanced at the clock on the wall, and his eyes literally popped out of his head. It was twenty past eleven! It couldn't be! He rushed into the bedroom. His wrist watch showed twenty-five past eleven.

He seized his head and groaned. A fine Sunday this, and as for the silage. . . .

Running out of the house, Anany Yegorovich was tempted to take the back ways, but at once dismissed this thought. What was the use of shuffling? By now, who wasn't aware that the kolhoz chairman was in bed recovering from a drunken bout?

The puddles gleamed, brimming with sunshine. His steps rang out like a tocsin in his ears. And the village looked dead. There wasn't even an urchin running across a street. . . .

It was clear. They'd all gone to the forest. Now he'd come to the end of the road.

"Comrades, look at this good-for-nothing chairman," the secretary of the district committee would say. "The Party entrusted a front-line sector to him, a matter of general importance for all the Soviet peoples at the moment. And what did he do? Help to spread drunkenness. . . ." And how would he justify himself? Nursing his toothache, should he say?

Unexpectedly the spluttering roar of a motor reached his ears. He stopped and listened. The machine was below, somewhere near the kolhoz office.

He ran to the top of a knoll. What he saw was an open truck with a huge load of hay crawling from the field gates, and a crowd of people in the meadow beyond the lake. People everywhere. With rakes and pitchforks. They were running about hoisting up the hay and staking it on carts.

He couldn't make head or tail of it. Had Isakov managed to do all this? Yes, only he could have done it. No one else. He must have arrived late last night from the district committee and started to swear and tear. And he had done all this while he, Anany, had been boozing away in the tearoom.

The truck drove up and out of the cab jumped Vasska Ouledev—his face perspiring, his white-toothed mouth open in a grin from ear to ear.

"Well, things are moving, chairman The folks are in a fine fury! The females dragged me straight out of bed. That's what thirty percent does for you!"

"Thirty percent?" Anany Yegorovich questioned dully.

"Well, of course. You said so yourself last night."

Vasska set his foot on the running board.

"I'm off. Today you can get it in the neck quick. The female population's gone on the rampage. I told them, 'Wait a while, the hay's still wet, let it dry a little.' 'Carry on,' they say, 'you tyrant. It's not your concern.' And that's true enough. For drying the hay, they're putting up all sorts of spikes—the men are building a shed by the stables. They think of everything."

"Keep your end up!" Vasska shouted from the cabin. "Isakov passed by not long ago with some other high-ups."

So that's what it was. The thirty percent. . . . But how could he have blurted out something like that? Why, they'd have his head for that. They'll say: "He's unleashed the instincts for private property. . . . The backward elements are guiding him by the reins. . . ." Anany Yegorovich set off to find Isakov. He must at least warn and inform him. "This is how it is," he'd say, "you'll have time to judge me, but in the meantime let's straighten out this mess."

. . . No, God strike him dead, but he couldn't remember it. He recalled everything. He remembered dropping into the tearoom, remembered everyone there: the brigadiers Chugayev, Obrosov, Voronitzin, Vasska Ouledev, Kirka-the-interpreter. . . . A whole session! He remembered their talking about Stalin's "little cows," that is, the goats which, after the war, pushed the cows out of the villages, remembered their arguments and vehemence about hay. . . . They'd talked of everything. But that he should have blurted out: "Stop idling. I give you thirty percent. . . ." Had he gone off his rocker? He hadn't even consulted with the management or the district committee.

Anany Yegorovich slowed his steps. "Maybe they've played a trick on me, the sons of bitches?" it suddenly struck him. "The chairman's drunk. Let him prove afterward that he didn't say it. . . ."

And however unlikely the notion, he was now ready to believe in it. The local kolhoz workers were capable of anything. He could expect anything from them. They had played a wicked joke on his predecessor, Martemyan Zykov. On arriving in the kolhoz, he had declared at his very first session: "I don't like messing about. I'll either raise the kolhoz level or you can cart me off to the cemetery." And would you believe it—within a year they'd carted him off. . . . One day the peasants had come across Martemyan—drunk and sprawling in the street. They bundled him into a small cart and carried him off to the cemetery. The man had been disgraced throughout the whole district. . . .

Another truck rushed past, rattling without a load. Yakov was at the wheel. His truck was fixed now. . . . Then he saw Petunya coming up behind the truck. Limping, he tramped along the middle of the road like a wood goblin. Steaming and sweating, he carried a rake and pitchfork over his shoulder.

129

"Something's wrong, chairman," he said, breathing heavily. "The brigadier's forgot his way to my place."

The old man had set off at a trot for the kolhoz office, from where the road stretched to the meadow; but then, evidently having decided to save time, he had taken a short cut.

And in the meadow. . . . All that was happening there! A multitude of white kerchiefs—far outnumbering the daisies; the heads of the peasants and the lads, heads of every color; and the urchins, like foals, tearing over green stubble of the reaped meadow. . . . Something about the scene reminded one of the early days of the kolhoz when the village still seethed with a surplus of energy.

"Yes," Anany Yegorovich sighed. "And all this is the result of thirty percent. Thirty percent. No sessions, no fuss, no noise."

Little by little he recovered. As he walked through a deserted street he thought: "What have I been afraid of? Why? So kolhoz workers would get a cow; so they would eat an extra spoonful of butter. Well, and what of it? Who would have benefited if the hay had been lost? And it would have been lost, lost for sure. Another day or two—and it would have been so much manure to cart from the meadow. And then everything would have gone to hell: the meat plan and the milk plan. And the harvest would have been buried under the snow too. It would have been total catastrophe!

"You know very well," Anany Yegorovich said to himself, "and you have known it for a long time, a kolhoz worker does his bit for the kolhoz when he owns a cow. But if he has no cow, he goes off kicking in every direction. Yes, to be honest, was that so fantastic—this thirty percent? Only last year they had paid up to forty percent in some districts—true, they weren't praised in the newspapers for that. Well, so what! You'll be hauled over the coals too. Maybe they'll even relieve you of the job. Maybe you'll get a good rapping through the district. Everything was possible. But, the devil take it, were you exerting yourself for your own sake? Remember all the blunders—not blunders, really, but rather the crimes committed in your time. Maybe you've forgotten all the twists and turns of the year 'thirty. . . . And the surplus appropriation after the war when, year after year, a clean sweep had been made of the kolhoz granaries? And the fact that almost as far north as the Polar region corn had been planted and then plowed under the rye? And you had understood all that, yes, you had understood and acted on it, forcing others to act that way too. You ought to have courage! If only once! If only this one time, at the age of fifty-five!"

Isakov lived in the sandy waste beyond the club. Isakov's house was distinguished by a tall poplar tree, and under it, from afar, Anany Yegorovich caught sight of the district committee *gazik*. This *gazik*—a new jeep with a canvas top—was usually driven by "him" in person, that is, by the first secretary, while the rest of the district committee workers used an old, rather battered jalopy.

"Yes," thought Anany Yegorovich, "that does it! If 'he' has driven in without any warning, he must have had a reason for it. Someone has let the cat out of the bag."

The sun was straight in his eyes. Rivulets of sweat ran down his unshaven face. He breathed heavily, raspingly—as if he were not walking over the familiar sandy waste so well trampled in every direction by many feet, but plowing virgin soil with his own feet.

The nearer he got to Isakov's house, the less courage remained. The accursed, uncontrolled fear, the old doubts about being right, alarm for his future and that of his family—all this was stifling him.

The windows of the house were wide open. A breeze stirred the white curtains. The radio blared festively, exultingly as befitted a Sunday (Isakov had his own radio). . . .

"Anany Yegorovich! Anany Yegorovich! . . ."

Mysovsky glanced around. Chugayev and Obrosov, the brigadiers, were running behind him, trying to catch up.

"Ha! the devil, we've been running like mad! We couldn't catch up with you," said Chugayev in his stride, wiping his face with the sleeve of his checked cowboy shirt. "What shall we do about the hay in the far meadows? The women are pressing us to go."

"There's no point waiting," Obrosov muttered gloomily.

Anany Yegorovich gritted his teeth. Here they were, his good friends of last night! They'd sat down to drink like men, but how had it all ended? It was as if they had sent him into a monastery. And as if to confirm this surmise, the sensitive Chugayev had glanced away like a thief when he had met the chairman's hard gaze. Suddenly he waved his arms.

"Look! Look! Over there! The allies!"

All three of them raised their heads. The cranes came flying very low over the village. They flew straight and began to hover in pairs above the meadow.

The cranes were seen in the meadow too. Joyful shouts, waving kerchiefs and rakes greeted them. According to local lore, cranes soared only in good weather—for that reason they had been nicknamed "allies."

"Well, what shall it be, chairman?" Chugayev asked again. A happy smile did not leave his round, pink face.

Obrosov stared without blinking at the chairman. He spoke more with his eyes. Anany Yegorovich suddenly licked his dry lips and glanced at Isakov's house. There was nobody at the windows. The radio stopped. It was as if the people behind the curtains were also sitting and waiting with bated breath for his decision.

"All right," he said slowly and firmly. "Send the people to the far meadows."

The black, shaggy brows on Obrosov's gaunt face quivered, and Chugayev, so it seemed, guiltily blinked his light blue eyes.

"Go on now!" exclaimed Anany Yegorovich.

Chugayev trotted after Obrosov. But suddenly he turned and, as if trying to cheer up his chairman, shouted:

"Don't worry about the silage now. It will all work out. You know how the people will shove on!"

Anany Yegorovich remained alone. His face was moist, but he himself was calm. Yes, he'd made his decision. He'd made it. And whatever happened, whatever might await him, nobody would be able to say that he'd issued a drunken order. A dog began to bark in Isakov's grass patch. Isakov and the secretary of the

district committee were descending the pale
blue steps bathed in sunshine.

Anany Yegorovich straightened his back and,
treading firmly on the sandy soil, went forward
to meet them.

FEMALE HOMOSEXUALITY: A modern study of Lesbianism
by Frank S. Caprio   BC-27   95¢
The most complete and authoritative work on its subject, this book is based on hundreds of interviews with lesbians, information gathered in travels around the world, and years of clinical research. It answers the need for a comprehensive study in non-technical language.

A MAN AGAINST INSANITY by Paul de Kruif   BB-28   60¢
The story of a doctor who conquered his own insanity and now shows others the way back, by the author of *Microbe Hunters*. "An old master Paul de Kruif surely is. His latest book has pace, it has style, it has a sharply drawn hero, and, most important, it tells one of the great stories of our times."—*Washington Post and Times Herald*.

BRIGHTER THAN A THOUSAND SUNS
by Robert Jungk   BC-29   75¢
The story of the men who made The Bomb, this is one of the most dramatic books ever published. "One of the most interesting books I have ever read. It is more exciting than any novel and, at the same time, it is packed with information which is both new and valuable."—Bertrand Russell

A LAYMAN'S GUIDE TO PSYCHIATRY
AND PSYCHOANALYSIS by Eric Berne   BC-30   75¢
What everybody should know about his mind and emotions: In simple and witty language, Dr. Berne explains the new science of human behavior. "This book is unique . . ."—Dr. A. A. Brill

THE NATURAL HISTORY OF LOVE
by Morton M. Hunt   BC-31   75¢
A brilliant panorama of the ways men and women have felt about love, from the early Greeks to the present day. ". . . a superbly written book . . . illuminating and clarifying for every reader."—*N. Y. Times Book Review*

REBEL WITHOUT A CAUSE by Robert M. Lindner   BC-32   75¢
The story of the analysis of a criminal psychopath, this brilliant book by a famed writer gave a name to a whole generation. "The most exciting and one of the most deeply and tragically human stories I have read in a long time."—*The New Republic*

THE AGE OF PSYCHOLOGY
by Ernest Havemann   BA-33   50¢
An invaluable layman's guide to the modern science of human behavior. In plain language it tells what scientists have discovered about our intelligence, emotions, and behavior.

THE PHYSIOLOGY OF MARRIAGE
by Honoré de Balzac   BC-43   75¢
A comprehensive and lighthearted discussion of infidelity in marriage by the great French novelist. It takes up in detail the general causes that bring all marriages to the crisis, its first symptoms, and the best policy for dealing with the crisis.

THE SWEET SCIENCE:
A Ringside View of Boxing by A. J. Liebling   BC-44   75¢
Joe Louis, Rocky Marciano, Archie Moore, Sugar Ray Robinson—all are here and many more. "This is not a book for fight fans alone; it is, to borrow a phrase, a hell of a piece of writing."—*San Francisco Chronicle*

VARIATIONS IN SEXUAL BEHAVIOR
by Frank S. Caprio, M.D.   BD-45   95¢
This complete study of deviations from approved sexual patterns, their causes and possible treatment is based on 30 years of psychiatric practice, treatment of so-called offenders, and testimony before courts, illustrated with case histories.

THE ABORTIONIST
by Dr. X as told to Lucy Freeman   BB-46   60¢
The first personal story ever published in America of the half-secret but always available world of abortion. "Miss Freeman's book should shake the puny little men who believe they are saving society when they hurl a skilled abortionist into prison."
—James A. Wechsler, *New York Post*

WORLD WAR I by Hanson W. Baldwin   BC-47   75¢
A compact, masterful history of the Great War by one of the most competent military analysts of our time. Surveying all theaters of the war, the book offers a previously unavailable perspective on this turning-point in modern history.

THE EVIL OF THE DAY by Thomas Sterling   BA-48   50¢
An elegant villa in Venice is the setting for a hoax that ends in murder. Unconventional characters and ironical plotting provide "one of the few practically perfect murder novels of the decade."—*New York Times*

THE AMERICAN SEXUAL TRAGEDY
by Albert Ellis   BD-49   95¢
A frank and detailed analysis of sex guilt by one of America's foremost psychologists and marriage counselors. "Millions of sexually confused people can find a guide to healthy living here. The prurient will damn it, and the repressed will run away from it. We wish it could be made compulsory for every couple. . . ."—Dr. Robert A. Harper in *Marriage and Family Living*

THE THREEPENNY OPERA
by Bertolt Brecht   BC-73   95¢

Complete text of the play which broke all box-office records in its six-year New York run. English book by Desmond Vesey; English lyrics by Eric Bentley. Includes author's notes and a foreword by Lotte Lenya.

KNOWLEDGE FOR WHAT?
by Robert S. Lynd   BC-74 $1.45

The classic work on the role of social science in American culture by the co-author of *Middletown* and *Middletown in Transition*. "The most searching volume in the annals of self-criticism in American social science."—Max Lerner.

THREE NOVELS BY SAMUEL BECKETT
BC-78 $1.45

First time in paperback! *Molloy, Malone Dies*, and *The Unnamable* form this trilogy. A major contribution to the modern novel, which has caused Beckett to be ranked along with Kafka and Joyce.

THE QUARE FELLOW & THE HOSTAGE
by Brendan Behan   BC-79 $1.45

Two full-length dramas by the famous Irish playwright, in one volume for the first time. "Behan is an astonishing man of the theater."—Walter Kerr.

THE JEWISH WIFE & OTHER SHORT PLAYS
by Bertolt Brecht   BC-80 $1.65

This volume includes *The Informer, In Search of Justice, The Exception and the Rule, The Measures Taken, The Elephant Calf*, and *Salzburg Dance of Death*.

BARRY GOLDWATER: Extremist of the Right
by Fred J. Cook   BC-81   75¢

The first book to take a critical look at the controversial Senator from Arizona. This hard-hitting book probes behind the headlines—and pulls no punches.

IMPOTENCE IN THE MALE, Vol. I
by Wilhelm Stekel, M.D.   BC-82   95¢

The first paperbound edition of this famous study of male impotence, its causes and cures. More than 120 fascinating case histories including such areas as vocations and sexuality, impotence and marriage, and impotence and religion.

IMPOTENCE IN THE MALE, Vol. II
by Wilhelm Stekel, M.D.   BC-83   95¢

The second volume of Dr. Stekel's world-famous study of male impotence covers war and impotence, impotence and criminality, and the end result of psychoanalytic cures.

SADISM AND MASOCHISM, Vol. I
by Wilhelm Stekel, M.D.   BC-85   95¢

This low-priced pioneering classic on the psychology of hatred and cruelty has been called, "The most complete and thought provoking book written on the subject of sadomasochism."—Emil Gutheil, M.D.